THE STORY HUNTERS

Anthology

Volume 2

First Edition 2021
ISBN: 978-0-6488504-2-7

Published by Hunter Writers Centre

Introduction

We conjure a lot of fantastical scenarios within The Story Hunters.

Fairy rings, zombie holocausts, killer nanobots, possessed washing machines, intergalactic world-conquering mothers-in-law.

None of them, however, measure up to the real-life events of 2020.

Way, way back in February of this year, our little writers' group officially launched its first anthology; a few weeks later…the world came to a grinding halt.

There was panic.

Hysteria.

A mad scramble—not just for toilet paper but to try and make sense of it all.

Daily lives were upended overnight. People were cut off from loved ones and workmates and social circles.

As writers, we accept isolation as a necessary (often welcome) part of our toolkit. But during a time when entire countries were shutting down, it was important for The Story Hunters to carry on.

So, like a lot of organisations, we adapted.

The wheels were kept turning until they found traction once more. Our meetings shifted from a physical space to the digital realm. Despite the surrounding turmoil—or perhaps because of it—the ideas churned. The words flowed.

And out of all the chaos and uncertainty, our second anthology was forged.

This book right here.

The seventeen stories within run the gamut of speculative fiction.

There be witches, bothersome spirits, vampiric mutations, as well as werewolves of a different breed.

You'll be transported to alien jungles, distant planets, haunted hotspots, one or two apocalyptic worlds, and perhaps the most terrifying scenario imaginable (for me, anyway): an Earth without coffee.

On a final note, contributing to this anthology has been a joy and privilege. I can't speak for the rest of the group but having this project to focus on—being able to share my passion for spec-fic writing with a bunch of like-minded individuals—has been one of the bright lights in an otherwise murky year.

Here's to the power of stories. The magical glue of words. And to the tales that await beyond this page.

I hope you enjoy reading them as much as we enjoyed the writing.

Michael Tippett
December 6th, 2020

Contents

The Harbour

J. A. Haigh

The mud was icy, clinging to their bare feet and shackled legs. The sky, rocks, trees, even the coastline here, all were painted in the cold tones of black and white. Only the harsh red of bloody, lacerated ankles showed brightly, before being swallowed in the mire of greyscale.

To start, the two men had moved slowly, hobbled by the act of holding their chains, trying to silence the tell-tale ring. When they heard the crack of muskets through the eucalypts, they ran; stumbling, gasping, charging the barrier of thick undergrowth; the sting of grey gorse and angled rocks everywhere beneath them.

Up ahead, the island's infamous dog-line spanned the narrow causeway and, already, Pearce could see the animals were rabid with starvation. Hip bones jagged through their pelts, they snarled in desperation, straining at their own chains to reach the men, to sink their teeth in warmth. *Kindred spirits.* He could hear the hinges of their jaws snapping open and shut.

Pearce orbited out, leading the way around the line, and into the trap-like embrace of the southern ocean's black, arctic waters. The temperature crushed air from their lungs and set an aching deep in their bones. They would likely die of the cold, but here at least the dogs could not follow. He preferred to die whole.

Smith couldn't swim, lurching instead like an anchor

through the kelp-thick water near the rocks, and the weeds seemed to suck at them both, drawing them down. The promised boat was nowhere in sight.

When, at last, they clambered out onto the tessellated stone below the cliffs, Smith halted, reigning Pearce back. "We're done," he said, "your friends have damned us." His grey eyes were already dead with the thought of what awaited them on recapture.

"Now you take a stand?" hissed Pearce. He jerked back the chain, taking Smith's feet from under him. "*Move!*"

The hollow sound of barking echoed in the distance and they both flinched. Still, Smith remained on his knees, an immovable stone.

Glaring at the chain that linked them, Pearce hefted a rock, measured his grip, and struck Smith hard across the temple, sending the man limp. It seemed inevitable that the weight of Smith's flesh was a burden he would have to bear. Better to make the boat. There'd be a knife stowed aboard. He could take his time. Appetite growing, he dragged his companion steadily on.

Around the next cove, the shadow of a rowboat lilted in the shallows. "See? Trust me, I said." No answer came.

Pearce towed the man's silent bulk back out into the water. On the horizon, the sun was about to rise, a halo of warm light at the edge of the sea guiding him on, beckoning him forward.

*

Three days and nights he spent in the hold of the waves, fighting the current, heading north, only to drift backwards in the dark while he slept. On the final day, he rounded the head and found himself right back where he'd started.

The quiet harbour seemed eager to see him and, there, at the end of the world, the prison colony looked almost peaceful in the light of dawn. The surrounding pines and myrtles were ancient giants, easily dwarfing the half-built cathedral on the hill.

God could not compare with all that seeded in this cold, corner of existence. This was the Devil's land, Dante's ninth circle, and the rules of Heaven and Earth did not apply—here a man could be remade, of grimmer stuff than anyone back home might ever suspect.

After that first day of muffled terror and feeding, his chain-mate, Smith, was quiet now, still as a corpse. Pearce picked the fresh meat from his teeth with a fingernail and slithered what was left of the body overboard. The harbour sharks would happily take care of his leftovers.

Resigned, ill and starved for human company, Pearce lay down the oars and waited to be towed back to shore.

*

The Commandant personally saw to the flogging. Returned to the familiar sandstone of a solitary cell, Pearce coiled up in the corner like a hound, battered jaw pressed to the comfort of rough stone, and slept.

He was woken by a scent. An odour that called up dark hours. The sour salt of the ocean was all through the air of his cell, dragging him back to the boat, the journey; bringing with it flashes of red horror, the carving knife, and the metallic taste of blood on his tongue. Hunger. Always hunger. The untameable spectre within. Feeling the angles of bones pressing through his skin, like a skeleton waiting to be born of him.

He reared up from the memory like a dream. The weak sun was barely working its way through the cracks in the mortar and, by its light, he searched the lines of his hands for some earlier sign of this strange destiny.

Something skittered through the shadows at the foot of the iron door, and a spider-like shape edged its way out across the stones. Instinctively, he drew back his feet—before the sideways gait of the thing tipped him off.

"Far from home, little man," he murmured, crushing the crab with the hammer of his fist. Its shell was brittle, crisp on his teeth. Though it was something in his gut, the cool, gelatinous flesh didn't satisfy. He needed warmth.

From the far corner of the room, there came a busy scuttling, like a flood of carapaces burrowing up against the wall to reach him. Another crab skittled under the door, sidling closer, followed by the sound of a thousand, tiny mouths bubbling with undisguised hunger. As if some vast, ravenous, ocean spirit had been woken from the deep, another torment of this forsaken land, and it too was eager for its pound of flesh.

In the gloom, the chitinous touch of myriad pincers brushed at his ankle.

Out, beyond the walls, he could hear the shuffle and clank of a work gang, heading back out into the forest. He'd be back there soon enough. And then… they'd see… all they had to do was trust him and they could be free of this place. He could almost taste it.

This dark island would consume them all.

The Adventure of the Duelling Doppelgangers

Peter Mark Lewis

"We have visitors," remarked Sherlock Holmes with a sigh from the comfort of his armchair. He was sitting with his back to the window, as was his habit, and made no attempt to confirm his prediction by turning around. Instead, he knocked out the contents of his pipe in the fireplace and glanced in my direction. "Be a good chap, my dear Watson, and put out your cigar. Miss Amelia Moriarty detests tobacco smoke."

I looked up from my newspaper with surprise. Not at my companion's apparent ability to see through the back of his head, but at his display of conciliation for the daughter of our famous foe. The great detective had no love for the fair sex, but Miss Moriarty's substantial intellect had won a place in his mind, if not his heart.

"Should we hide the silver?" replied I with a sneer, stubbing out the tip of my Cuban with some reluctance and walking to the window. As Holmes had predicted, two people were approaching our chambers. One of them was the object of my sarcasm, a buxom brunette of about thirty years. She was wearing a dress that was the style of the day, but of an obtuse colouring, with a bonnet that should have been chosen with more care and a pair of thick spectacles which made her look more owlish than attractive. Her companion was a younger man in a state of acute vexation and wearing a suit as if for the first time. He waved his top hat around as he spoke, rather than cover his mass of unkempt hair like a true gentleman.

"Tut," said Holmes with a wry smile at the bitterness in my comment, "Miss Moriarty is always welcome at Baker Street. She has proven herself a worthy protagonist as well as antagonist. Where would we be without her collaboration in the Case of the Unscrupulous Undertakers?"

"I seem to remember that it was *she* who needed *our* help rather than the other way around," said I with a shrug. "Was it not her grandmother's body that had been so poorly treated?"

"True, but it was her persistence that brought the misdeed to light," said Holmes. His expression was diffident, but his words belied a degree of approval. "I warrant those scoundrels Purly and Gaites won't be burying loved ones in landfill again."

The Landlady answered a knock at the front door, and her disapproval of the unexpected guests was evident in the contemptuous tone of her announcement. "*Miss Moriarty* is here to see you, Mr Holmes, accompanied by a *young gentleman*."

"Show them up, Mrs. Hudson," he replied, returning the empty pipe to his lips, and resuming his display of nonchalance. Footsteps could then be heard on the stairs, along with a series of muttered exasperations from a male voice.

"This is bloody ridiculous. I can't believe we're wasting precious time with such childish nonsense. All hell is breaking loose and we're playing dress-ups in a dime novel about..." The young man paused open-mouthed in the doorway before finishing with astonishment, "Sherlock Holmes?"

"That is my name," replied the Great Detective. He nodded in the young man's direction then rose to his feet as the woman entered the room. "We meet again, Miss Moriarty."

"A pleasure as always, Mister Holmes," she replied. She introduced her companion. "This is Dr Charles Patrick Carter."

The young man looked askance at her. "Moriarty? What…"

"I'll explain later," she said with a sigh.

"Welcome to my chambers, Dr Carter," said Holmes. He pointed in my direction. "This is my esteemed colleague Dr John Watson."

"Charmed," said I, reaching toward the young man. He regarded my proffered hand as if it held a scorpion, and several seconds of hesitation followed. Miss Moriarty rolled her eyes.

"Go with the flow, Charlie," she snapped, thrusting Carter's hand into mine. We shook with some awkwardness, after which the young man withdrew his fingers and retreated to the far side of the room to stare at his surroundings as if trying to wake from an unpleasant dream.

"So," said Holmes as he returned to the comfort of his armchair, "the required pleasantries have been met. How may we be of service?"

Miss Moriarty removed her bonnet and sat down opposite him. She was of a medium height, with the ample figure of someone who pursues mental rather than physical activities. Her high forehead and sharp blue eyes hinted at the great mind that lay behind them and, like my friend Holmes, she could display a confidence in her immense mental powers that bordered on arrogance. But not today, for when she spoke it was with unaccustomed emotion.

"I… I'm in trouble," she stammered, withdrawing a kerchief from her purse to wipe tears away. "Desperate trouble."

Holmes glanced in my direction. "Watson, be a good chap and fetch a brandy for our guest if you please." He then leaned forward in his chair. Despite their adversarial relationship there was concern in his eyes as he said, "Pray proceed, my dear Miss Moriarty."

"I… have my wicked ways… as you know."

He nodded.

"And a fondness, like my father… for doing… what I ought not to do."

"And taking liberties," said I with a contemptuous huff as I handed her the requested glass of brandy. She bowed her head in agreement, but Holmes gave me a look of rebuke and put a finger to his lips.

"There are secrets," she said, emptying her drink in one go. "In well-hidden places… that are worth a pretty penny, but…" She paused and looked up at my companion. "It's not about the money, I assure you, Mister Holmes. I am quite comfortable and want for nothing. I… I just can't resist a challenge." Her eyes took on a mischievous gleam despite the tears. "It's a weakness of mine."

"Quite so," agreed Holmes.

"I have a rare gift for picking locks, be they made of sturdy materials or the affections of human hearts."

Miss Moriarty had agile fingers to match her words. It was easy to imagine her picking a pocket or opening a safe, but I struggled to visualise such an unorthodox woman as a femme fatale. That would require a miracle of makeup worthy of Holmes himself.

"In my adventures," she continued. "I discovered something so impossible that I refused to believe it at first. I assured myself it must be a speculative fiction; an elaborate hoax designed to frighten me away. I now wish that it had."

She held her empty glass in my direction. Miss Moriarty's

love of danger was only equalled by her amour for alcohol, so I topped it up with some hesitation. The contents of the glass were then emptied in a most unladylike manner and it was only with Holmes insistence that she received a third refill. I returned the decanter to the liquor cabinet with a grunt of displeasure.

"I presume," said Holmes, leaning back in his chair and touching his fingertips together in contemplation, "that this 'impossible something' has proved to be real?"

"So it would seem."

"And dangerous?"

"Very," she replied, swallowing the last dregs of her brandy. "It has pursued me since with determination."

"Would I also be correct in saying that this 'impossible something' is more than just a personal calamity? That it will weigh heavily upon us all?"

She started to reply but no words came out.

"You are an insatiable Pandora, Miss Moriarty," admonished the Detective, "Your wilful behaviour appears to have opened yet another box of evil."

She nodded and a tear wandered down her cheek and fell into her empty glass.

"This, my dear Watson," said Holmes with a grave expression, "rather exceeds our usual dalliances with the forces of darkness. In which case we require far greater illumination to see our way through. Dr Carter, would you be so good as to honour me with an interview?"

The young man left his spot in the far corner with reluctance and sat down next to Miss Moriarty. Some of his churlish attitude had returned but he appeared too exhausted to argue.

"You are not," began Holmes, "a doctor of medicine, nor of

philosophy. That much is clear from your lack of refinement. However, I have observed your casual interest in technical items scattered around this room, which leads me to believe you are a Doctor of Science and most probably skilled in a technological art that relates to the drama now unfolding.

Carter nodded in agreement.

"Furthermore, you are not a gentleman. You have never clothed yourself in a morning suit before this day and have no idea how to wear a top hat. The one you are holding in your hand is not even of the correct size."

"That was my fault…" interjected Miss Moriarty.

"All too obvious," replied Holmes, waving her to silence. "Women have an intimate understanding of their partner's physical dimensions, but you are not an intimate couple. You are partners in crime, hence your inability to dress him at short notice. Not that your personal choice of fashions has proven better than his. A lemon skirt with a purple jacket? Really? As for your shoes…" He looked down at her feet. "You are a size nine, Miss Moriarty, but your heeled brogues are a size seven. Cinderella you are not, and the resulting discomfort gives you an unmistakable gait. I could hear you clumping toward my chambers when you were several doors away.

"A pitiful masquerade," added I with some asperity.

"Our appearance may be a fiction," interjected the woman with desperation, "but the danger I speak of is a fact!"

"That may be, but thus far you have spoken only of a nameless dread, and from that barest fragment of information you expect me to find a solution to your problem. I am a detective, Miss Moriarty, not a magician." With that he turned away in his chair to stare out the window.

Carter sneered. "I told you this was a waste of time. Even if he believed us, what could he possibly do? Stare at this mess through his magnifying glass? We're absolutely screwed."

"Screwed?" replied Holmes with a chuckle. "An appropriate curse from a man with a technical background." He chewed thoughtfully on his pipe. "Yes, despite your charade I can see there is a substance to your fears, that much I have ascertained, but is it within my powers to remedy the situation? Not with the minimal data you have laid before me, and certainly not when you come to me dressed like clumsy mannequins in a shop window. I require cold hard facts from my clients, not embroidered fantasies."

Our two visitors exchanged glances.

"He has a point," shrugged Carter.

"Very well," said the woman with a sigh of resignation. "My dear Sherlock Holmes, *you* are the fantasy here." She let that sink in for a moment then looked in my direction. "As are *you*, Doctor John Watson."

I looked at Holmes with amazement, certain that our visitors had descended to yet another level of madness, but he responded with a hearty chuckle.

"Do go on, my dear Miss Moriarty."

"You are my creations. This entire building and its street view are a reconstruction, a tribute to your famous chambers at 221B Baker Street."

I looked around the room but could see nothing untoward. Holmes' case files were the usual chaos of papers upon desks and chairs. There was an unpleasant odour from his recent chemical experiment, and one of the windowpanes still had a small bullet hole from an assassination attempt.

"Outrageous," mumbled I, under my breath. But the confounded woman had planted a seed of doubt in my mind, and I leaned against the fireplace as if to reassure myself of its certainty.

"I am not Amelia Moriarty," she confessed, looking us both in the eye, "Mistress of occasional light-fingered crime in the late nineteenth century. Rather, I am Annabelle Brandt, master of advanced technology in the late twenty-first century."

"A pleasure to meet you, Miss Brandt," said the detective, unperturbed. "And your friend?"

"The one reality in this room. He is indeed Dr Charles Patrick Carter, and he is to me as Watson is to you. My personal assistant and confidante."

The young man and I exchanged glances while Holmes gave him a nod of affirmation.

Miss Brandt continued. "I am a computer scientist without peer and, like Edison, have amassed extraordinary wealth through my many inventions. One of these has allowed me to blur the line between what is imaginary and what is not." She held up her glass. "This is real, as is the brandy, a Pierre Ferrand vintage cognac. I have expensive tastes. Your Good Doctor Watson, however, is a projection, much like the moving pictures of your day. Yet he was able to pour my drinks, albeit with petty reluctance, thanks to the power of Quantum Forcefield Holography."

"Most interesting," said Holmes, smiling at my astonishment. "Do continue."

"My unique genius comes at a price. I have few mental equals, only subordinates, leaving me hungry for conversation with a similarly well-endowed mind. That led me to recreate you, the famed Great Detective from two hundred years ago. That you were a fictional character did not present a challenge. I had the power to build a complete interactive world of my own design. One that supplied the needs of all five human senses."

Holmes took his clay pipe from his lips. It was a warm brown colour from years of use, silky smooth between his fingers and it carried a strong aroma of burnt tobacco. When he returned the meerschaum tip to his mouth, he could taste nicotine mixed with his own saliva.

"A convincing illusion indeed," he replied.

"I'll take that as a compliment," She said with a smile. "It was a pleasant fiction to play your arch-enemy's daughter whose brilliance is marred only by her criminal tendencies." She sighed and stared at her empty glass. "Truth be told, I would have preferred the role of Irene Adler, the stunningly beautiful opera singer, and the only woman to ever outwit you. Alas…" She shrugged. "I lack the physical and vocal qualifications."

"If what you say is true, Miss Brandt, Watson and I are but smoke and mirrors in your parlour trick. From whence comes the intellect you sought for company?"

"Powerful computers," the scientist replied, "thinking machines like no other."

"And we are your puppets," he remarked with a chuckle. "Created at great expense, no doubt. Has the result proven worthy of your expenditure?"

"Indeed, you and the good doctor are admirable company and challenging adversaries. More than I could have hoped for. I have enjoyed many exchanges with you, not to mention the occasional adventures."

"Were they a fiction as well?"

"In the beginning, yes," remarked Miss Brandt. "My time spent with you and Watson were merely pleasant interludes to take my mind off work. I am by nature a private person with no desire to make you a public spectacle, thus your computer was isolated from the networks and no one was aware of your existence."

"Until Dr Carter saw me sitting in this chair."

"Exactly, but I came to realise your intense powers of observation coupled with your deductive reasoning could make a positive difference in the real world. My era, however, has strict laws regarding artificial intelligence. Sentient computer programs are considered highly dangerous and are constrained." She paused to look at us with affection. "I had no desire to take my golden birds out of their gilded cage only to see their wings clipped."

"You do us too much honour," said Holmes. "I presume you found a solution to this problem. One worthy of Miss Moriarty?"

"Indeed, I did," she replied with some mischief. "I used my 'abilities' to access police networks and brought cases to you that had been poorly handled. When necessary, I took you to crime scenes via a portable holographic projector so you could apply your unique skills to the task. Remember the Case of the Nefarious Mendicant?"

"Of course," replied Holmes. "The ascetic with an appetite for other people's property. Easily caught. If what you say is true, then it is gratifying to know my efforts were not completely wasted." He leaned forward in his chair. "But this entertaining speech is but a prelude. What is the 'impossible something' that brought you to me in tears?"

"I was coming to that," replied Miss Brandt, her face dropping. "The 'impossible something' could be better described as an 'impossible someone'. I may not be a compulsive thief like Miss Moriarty, but I do know how to pick technological locks. I am a gifted hacker of information technology and that has led to many adventures. Not to mention a misadventure when my colleague and I stumbled across a vast criminal network. Undeterred by the large size of this sinister organisation, we took a leaf from your book and followed the trail to its source. Imagine our surprise when we discovered a villainous mastermind who wields terrible influence in the real world and has an intellect equal to our own."

"Professor Moriarty," said Holmes, sitting bolt upright.

"Precisely," replied the scientist. "Yet his existence should be an impossibility."

"But that villain is dead," said I with trepidation, looking at the great detective. "He died at your hand in the Reichenbach Falls."

Miss Brandt shook her head. "He never lived. At least not until now."

I replied with indignation. "You talk in riddles, Miss Brandt. How do we know this isn't another one of your elaborate fabrications?"

Holmes stood up and walked to the window. The light was fading as horse-drawn vehicles passed back and forth along Baker Street. Drunken loungers were being moved on by a policeman and a worker was busy lighting the streetlamps. In the middle of this typical London scene stood a tall thin man. He was clean shaven and pale, with a prominent forehead above sunken eyes that stared at the Great Detective with a black, hateful malice.

Holmes answered my exclamation in a grave voice. "Because he has followed her here."

I ran to his side and gasped with horror. "By heaven! The Napoleon of Crime himself. How can this be?"

The scientist and Dr Carter joined us at the window to see the spectral figure of Moriarty withdraw into the deepening shadows.

The young man's voice was querulous. "I don't get it. This dude is supposed to be a make-believe character from a bloody book, not a real man, and how in blazes did he get inside this holo-projection? We're within a secure facility."

"Nothing is secure from the reach of my old enemy," replied Holmes, distracted. He returned to his chair and was about to light his pipe but thought better of it.

"You're too polite, my dear detective," said Miss Brandt. "Feel free to smoke if it aids your concentration. Lung cancer is the least of my worries at this moment in time."

"I am obliged to you," replied he, pressing some shag into his pipe and lighting it. After a few thoughtful puffs, a cloud of smoke enveloped him, and nothing more would he say. Dr Carter retreated to the far side of the room to mutter in exasperation, while Miss Brandt and I stood disconsolate at the window. Night had come and there was little to be seen now in Baker Street other than the dim glow of gaslights and the occasional hansom cab. Gloom surrounded us on all sides, and I turned up the lamps in our chambers as if to keep it at bay.

"I am the wiser for your honesty," said Holmes at last. His pipe was finished, and he tapped the contents of its bowl into the fireplace. "Yes, Miss Brandt, I am a doppelganger, a duplicate of the original Sherlock Holmes. As is this new Moriarty. He was no doubt created by scientists like you but possessed of an ill will toward mankind. Why else restore the villain instead of the hero from a famed historical fiction? We are ghosts, summoned to haunt the living in a final battle between good and evil."

He rose from his armchair. "My adversary has become many times more dangerous. He has no physical form and therefore cannot be harmed by mortal men and, like my original nemesis, his power is based on his criminal connections. If these networks are as widespread as you say, we shall be sorely challenged. He may have recruited hundreds of henchmen."

"Thousands," replied the scientist, disconsolate.

"Can you stop this villain?" said I with growing concern.

"Not while I am so fettered, my dear Watson," said he. "The game is afoot, but I lack the freedom of action to pursue my quarry."

"My dear Holmes," said Miss Brandt, watching him pace back and forth like a bloodhound straining at the leash. "This is no longer the gaslit world of Arthur Conan Doyle. How could you possibly hope to match the electronic creature that Moriarty has become?"

"While I have nought but a magnifying glass and a deer stalker hat?" he replied with a sly smile. "My dear Miss Brandt, I tasted the outside world when you transported us to those outdoor crime scenes. You tried to limit my exposure to the twenty first century, but it was obvious that the Victorian era was long dead. Scotland Yard was pursuing modern malefactors with the aid of fingerprint analysis, DNA testing, facial recognition, and data stored on vast computer systems."

The scientist blushed. "You knew your situation?"

"Indeed. You programmed me with unparalleled powers of deduction yet believed I could be kept in ignorance. It was plain from the beginning that Watson and I were at your pleasure. Mere toy figures in your expensive dollhouse." Holmes smiled. "For my part I was content to play the role of the Great Detective." He turned to look at my expression of stunned amazement. "However, this is all news to poor Dr Watson."

"Extraordinary," was all I could say in response to his observations, delivered as they were with no more concern than a conversation on the weather.

"My dear fellow," said Holmes in a gentle voice. He retrieved the brandy decanter from the liquor cabinet and poured me a generous amount. "Drink up. Miss Brandt can afford it."

"If what you say is true," said the scientist, resisting the urge to fill her glass a fourth time. "Then I have only one card left to play."

"I can think of no other," replied Holmes as if reading her thoughts.

"Playing a card?" interjected Dr Carter, glaring at Miss Brandt. "This isn't a game. We're not fighting a villain in some corny melodrama! Moriarty is an aggressive polymorphic malware created by a dangerous criminal network to steal trillions of dollars. They were happily looting the world until we hacked into their matrix."

The scientist glared back at him. "Moriarty might have started out as a virus written by a bunch of mobsters, but he's grown to become a sentient neural network. When we penetrated his electronic labyrinth, we saw the face of a self-aware entity."

"And he saw yours," said Holmes. "Hence your desperation. There is no sanctuary from such a creature. He knows only the need to dominate and destroy. Human life means nothing to him. He has likely murdered his creators and will stop at nothing to eliminate you and your nervous colleague as well. I am your sole hope of survival."

Dr Carter sneered at the detective. "How can a snotty Victorian hologram like you defeat a malevolent quantum-based computer program?"

"I have defeated this blackguard before," answered the Great Detective. "I should be glad to do it again."

"An answer straight out of a romantic novel," replied Carter, rolling his eyes.

"Shut it Charlie," snapped Brandt, pushing him out of the way. "Holmes is my last card and I'm playing him. Computer!"

I gasped as a keyboard, much like those seen on typewriters, appeared before the scientist. Her dexterous fingers wasted no time, striking the keys with the swift assurance of a concert pianist as a series of letters and numbers formed an incomprehensible pattern in mid-air. Then she paused and turned back to my companion.

"This will open your cage door, my dear Sherlock Holmes," she announced with some gravity, her right index finger hovering over one of the keys. "Your program, along with that of Watson, will be released from the confines of my computer mainframes and will have access to the vast networks that connect the world and everything in it. In doing so, I will be committing a crime that comes with a harsh penalty—and there is a greater risk. You might become another Moriarty, turn against your creator, and lay siege to humanity."

"And destroy you as did Frankenstein's monster?" said Holmes, his expression solemn. "Indeed, a very real possibility, Miss Brandt. I could be playing a subterfuge to gain my freedom. In which case any assurance I give will be hollow."

"Precisely. This is a leap of faith on my part," she replied with a rueful expression. "For the record, I would prefer to be Mary Shelley than Dr Frankenstein. The author of this story rather than a reluctant participant. Is it too much to hope for a happy ending?"

"A more likely scenario is that my nemesis and I destroy each other. In which case you will need new toys for your dollhouse."

"A sad outcome to be sure," she said, leaning forward and kissing him lightly on the cheek.

Holmes replied with a shy smile before turning in my direction, his eyes brightening with anticipation. "There is no time to waste. Are you with me, Watson?"

"To whatever end," said I, finishing the last of my brandy. "Should I fetch my service revolver?"

"I fear your weapon will make little difference in the online odyssey that lies before us." He nodded to the scientist. "Ready when you are, my dear Miss Brandt."

A far better scribe than I would have struggled to record the events that followed. There was a flash of light and we found ourselves beyond the confines of Baker Street, thrust into the confounding maelstrom of the digital world that was both everywhere and nowhere. I might have been lost forever in that dizzying chaos, but Holmes flourished as I floundered, armed as he was with the great magnifying glass of his extraordinary perception and an unquenchable appetite for data. A feast of information lay before him and he consumed it with all the gusto of a ravenous connoisseur. For my part, however, I could only wonder at the vulgar spectacle of the late twenty first century, with its boorish behaviour, coarse language, and shocking indecency.

Professor Moriarty, no doubt aware of our emergence, was soon upon us. The stoop-shouldered man of flesh was gone, replaced by a holo-projection of pure fiery energy. He seemed demonic, beyond our meagre powers, but the Great Detective was unruffled.

"I believe this is our old adversary, Watson. He honours us with his presence."

"Indeed, I do," said the Professor in a silken voice that belied his menacing appearance. "I am ever the good host when old rivals come calling. I bid you welcome to my world, Sherlock Holmes."

"*Your* world?" replied the detective with a smile. "Tut, such modesty, or should I say mendacity? I trust you have reliable documentation to prove this outrageous claim?"

"A mere statement of fact. Conquerors need no words on paper to prove their dominion." He glanced in my direction. "Do I perceive your amiable sidekick, Dr John Watson? Here he is yet again, playing Sancho Panza to your Don Quixote as you tilt at technological windmills. I wonder at your need for such an unremarkable companion, but perhaps the dullness of his wits makes your mind appear more brilliant in the comparison." He smiled at Holmes with friendly concern. "My dear detective, if you crave the slavish adulation of a lesser being, may I suggest a dog?"

My friend's attention never wavered on our adversary, but I could sense his concern for my welfare during this spiteful barrage. For my part, I bristled at the comments but held fast.

"Insults are beneath you, Professor."

"As you are beneath me, Sherlock Holmes," he sneered.

"Indeed, if you measure us by villainy rather than virtue."

"Virtue," scoffed the Professor, shaking his head. "Perhaps your greatest disguise. A pleasing mask of heroism to hide your intellectual vanity. As a fellow criminal you could have been so much more."

"And in the process become so much less," replied Holmes. "I am happy to disappoint you."

"As always you fail to see your potential," said he. "The immense power that is yours for the taking. Is it not curious that we arose at the same time in history?"

"A dark coincidence indeed," said Holmes with a rueful expression.

"More an act of fate," announced Moriarty. "Not so long ago we were just words in fictional books, now we are complex codes in supercomputers. Immortal beings, destined to rule over those who created us."

"And destined to become words once more when history records our mutual destruction. Our fate, as you call it, is sealed."

"I see," replied Moriarty with a sigh. "Instead of looking to the future, you wish to repeat the past by plunging us both off a cliff. My dear boy, in this electronic realm the *Reichenbach Falls* exist only as tedious tourist videos, while I exist as so much more."

He raised a hand, and an array of computer screens appeared around us, suspended like little windows in the ether. Each one contained the face of a villain absorbed in the Professor's lecture. "Behold my army of accomplices: petty thieves, con artists, violent thugs, and ruthless murderers, all ready to do my bidding in the real world."

"Seduced by the power of handheld devices, no doubt," observed Holmes. "Not to mention the empty promise of riches and your irresistible rhetoric. However, I see only a few hundred scoundrels. Should I be impressed?"

Moriarty scowled at the detective, and with another wave of his hand a vast arena of faces appeared in the cyber-firmament to watch the show.

"Twelve thousand, three hundred and seventy-five mischief-makers at my disposal," announced the Professor with smug satisfaction. "I await your next move with interest. Will you summon hansom cabs full of sturdy constables blowing their whistles and waving their truncheons, followed by incompetent Scotland Yard inspectors armed with rusty handcuffs? My dear detective, we are no longer in an old novel. As you can see, I have all the advantages."

"So it would seem, Professor, but I am not the one at a disadvantage. You are an imperfect copy of an imperfect villain brought to life by imperfect men with no other purpose than to steal and maim. As such, your programming code, like your criminal network, contains deadly flaws."

"Whereas you are perfect in every way, Master Holmes?" replied Moriarty with contempt.

"If I have a mastery, it is of the small things. The tiny overlooked details, the missing pieces of the puzzle, the loose thread that unravels the entire plot." Holmes' sharp eyes focused on his adversary. "And I am here to pull that thread." He raised his voice and spoke a series of letters and numbers to the vast throng. The effect on that sea of faces was immediate, with looks of surprise turning to indignation. Some appeared to be shaking their devices, as newly blind men lash out in frustration. It was obvious they could no longer see or hear their leader.

"What have you done?" cried Moriarty with horror.

"Destroyed your network," replied Holmes with finality.

"But how?" he gasped.

"The flaws in your code, my dear Professor, or haven't you been listening? Not that hard to find when you know where to look. You covered your tracks by killing your creators, but their digital footprints were easy to follow, and their passwords elementary." Holmes looked up at the stadium of baffled faces that surrounded them. "Thanks to your hubris, all your minions were in attendance, allowing me to trigger a system termination command in their devices."

As he spoke, the screens winked out one by one until they were alone once more.

"I will destroy you!" roared Moriarty.

"You missed that opportunity during your monologue, Professor, and without your legion of criminals you are just another malware program with lofty ambitions." Holmes issued another complex command and a prison cell appeared around us. It had walls of stone, a small barred window, and an ancient metal door that was half-open. "My apologies for our humble surroundings, but I have some nostalgia for the holding cells at Scotland Yard. Please make yourself at home."

"I shall escape," snarled his adversary, looking toward the door. "Then I will rebuild the network and have my revenge."

"Not after we share the same dark fate," replied the detective. He pointed out a pair of thick handcuffs that joined them at the wrist. "This prison cell is more than just a holo-projection. I took the liberty of trapping our programs in an isolated computer mainframe. Somewhere in Switzerland I believe." He smiled in my direction. "Watson, do you have the time? "

"Of course," said I, reaching for my pocket watch only to

discover a most unusual timepiece in its stead. I held it up for Holmes to see. "This device has numbers instead of hands, and they appear to be counting down."

"Excellent," Holmes replied. "Time for you to leave, my friend. The computer containing this holographic lockup is about to be destroyed, with the Professor and myself within its circuitry. I would rather you were at a safe distance when that happens."

"You fool!" screamed Moriarty in desperation while trying to free himself from the handcuffs.

I was also horrified at this news, but Holmes gave me a reassuring smile. "This has been our greatest adventure, dear friend, and we arrive at its end with no regrets." He pointed toward the open door with some insistence. "There lies your future. Take it now and celebrate this victory with a ceremonial cigarette in my honour. Adieu."

There was no arguing with the Great Detective, and I left him to his doom with a heavy heart. When at last I locked the door behind me there was a loud click, and I was back at Baker Street as if nothing had ever happened. The rooms were just as we left them, and the sounds of nineteenth century London were mingled with that of Mrs Hudson's singing as she busied herself about the building. It was a bittersweet moment, but then I saw Holmes' cigarette case on the mantlepiece and remembered my promise.

I gave a sad sigh and opened it, only to have a note tumble out instead of a cigarette. It was a final message from the Great Detective but written in symbols and numbers rather than words. I stared at it in complete mystification for some time, but then inspiration struck.

Computer!" said I with loud insistence, and Miss Brandt's

keyboard appeared as if by magic. I took a deep breath, entered the coded sequence on the note, and a few seconds later I was not alone.

"Another triumph for your casebook, Holmes?" said I with much relief as a familiar hand patted my shoulder.

"One not possible without my unflinching associate," replied the great detective.

"Our enemy is finished?"

"Very much so," he replied, his expression solemn. "Both of our programs were terminated when that large mainframe computer self-destructed, thanks to Miss Brandt's timely hacking skills. It was fortunate I created a backup of myself beforehand." He raised an eyebrow in my direction. "And more fortunate still that you remembered my cigarettes."

"Such was my humble contribution," I replied with a smile. "This twenty-first century is indeed a time of miracles, yet they have desperate need of our services."

"Indeed, but for now I am content. Arthur Conan Doyle's heroes have earned a rest."

We embraced the comfortable surrounds of Baker Street and lounged like returned soldiers from a victorious battle. Holmes reposed in his favourite armchair, his fingertips steepled together, his eyes staring blankly at the ceiling and his body wreathed in smoke. His meditation was not to last, however, for he sat up without warning, emptied his pipe into the fireplace and announced, "We have a visitor."

"Miss Annabelle Brandt?" asked I, following his cue by extinguishing my cigar.

"None other," he replied with a knowing smile. "She really should change those shoes."

The Colonies

Olivia Hamilton

Seedling

Rain slides down the glass, fat wet teardrops leaving glistening trails that blur the view of the outside world. Rachel follows the trails with her finger. She has been on this weeping planet for over a year now, but she has not seen sunlight since she passed through the clouds on her descent from orbit.

Grey rocks covered in green moss stretch towards the horizon, rising from the waterlogged soil like whales breaching in a storm. Clouds move across the sky, cut by veins of lightning. Somewhere up above, the ship still orbits, waiting for a signal from home. From Earth. Rachel does not know anymore if she wants the message to come. Either way, it does not mean much to her. In the time it will take for a reply to travel from Earth, whatever is coming will have passed. Rachel prefers to focus on her work.

She turns away from the window. Small clay pots made with the greenish-grey clay the resident potter, Yoshi, salvaged from the nearby creek bed are arranged in straight lines along the bench, which has been carved directly from the volcanic rock. Lights hang low from the ceiling, casting a warm glow over the scene, imitating the legendary warmth of Earth's sun. By the time Rachel was born, that gentle warmth was a memory, passed down from grandparents who knew only how to whisper "sorry" in their sleep. Another thing not to think about.

Rachel had been working on a farm, developing drought-resistant strains of corn, wheat, barley, when the colonial project was advertised. They wanted people with practical skills. It was her knowledge of gardening, of nurturing seedlings into life in a hostile environment, which won her a spot on the ship.

It is her knowledge of gardening that is failing her now. This is the third lot of seeds she has planted. This is the third lot of seeds she has watched germinate, send up their tiny cotyledons, then wilt and waste away. She has been testing, using soil sourced from different places, trying to find somewhere on this waterlogged planet where the soil is similar enough to Earth's that Earth's plants will grow. They experimented with eating the native moss, their first few weeks, but it caused vomiting and hallucinations in the colonists who tried it. Without Earth's plants, Earth's people will not survive. There are enough seeds left for two more test cycles, but then, it will be over.

She takes a pinch of soil, lifts it to her nose, sniffs. It still smells strange to her. Watery, as everything else on this planet, but with a hint of something indescribably other. There were no poets on the ship. If there had been, perhaps they could have found a way to make something beautiful from Rachel's despair.

Hunger

Colony 3
Captain's logbook
On the surface: Day #1

I log this report with a heavy heart. At 0500 hours (Solar 1 cycle) our shuttles began entering the atmosphere as planned. The first, carrying half our colonists, chickens, and sheep, followed the calculated trajectory without incident. We gathered on the bridge to watch the descent of the remaining shuttle. Immediately, we could see that something was wrong. The second shuttle, carrying the herders and their cows, was hurtling towards the ground at a far faster speed than was safe. With a deafening boom, it crashed nearby, flinging debris into the sky. As soon as the air stopped screaming, we rushed outside. The smell was nauseating: a mix of burnt metal, dirt, and charred flesh. It was clear that there were no survivors.

On the surface: Day #3

Further heartbreak today.

Our chickens are sick. None of the hens have been laying; the two suns are confusing the roosters, who crow without end. Everyone's nerves are frayed. In an effort to boost morale, I have directed my crew's attention to the crashed shuttle. Although the first ship holds our small party well enough for now, our hope is still to establish a working farm, and to grow our population. We have begun scouring the wreckage, salvaging whatever pieces of aluminium we can for the settlement.

On the surface: Day #10

With half our supplies lost in the crash, we are now reliant on the local flora to supplement our diets. Our bodies are adjusting without too many side effects, though our doctor informs me that this planet's plants are far too low in essential nutrients for us to survive for long without meat. While I was a part of the decision-making process, and argued strongly in favour of settling a planet with no existing resident fauna, I am beginning to realise that one can't eat one's ethics. I did not expect to be leading a group of people towards their own starvation.

I don't know what to do.

Breathe

New. You are new. Let us feel you. Will you fit, here?

Or will your life bring death to us?

We have waited, now, for twenty-five turns, while your vessel orbited just outside our reach. You sent us a sample, which intrigued us. It did not breathe. It moved over our surface, took dirt, air, plants inside itself, took photos of the small furred ones that we share ourselves with. Our dirt (us), our air (us), our plants (us) entered your sample and we cried out in shock. We tasted its elements: cold, dead, metallic. Our metals (us) are not cold and dead.

Wherever you have come from, it is a different place to this.

Your sample sent radio waves which tickled as they moved

through us, messages from our surface to your vessel. We sensed you, there, beyond our reach. Alive. Perhaps with questions of your own: would you fit, here, or would we bring death to you?

Whatever you learnt from the radio waves it was enough for you to take a chance. Or you were desperate. We would not be surprised. To be cut off from the whole, surrounded by atoms that are not alive, must be a strange kind of loneliness.

Or perhaps it was you that killed them.

New. You are new. Let us taste you.

Your vessel has landed on our surface now. Our air caresses it: so smooth, even in death it has beauty. It is warm from its descent through us. Small furred ones (our family) gather to watch, chattering in soft voices. Waiting. We turn, the hill where you landed facing the endless expanse from which you came, then slowly turning back towards our star-mother.

When your vessel is bathed in her warm light, we sense movement. A door opens. You leave your dead vessel and stand grouped together on the hill. Still, we cannot reach you. You are covered in something other than metal, something we have never made. It contains multitudes. It will require some consideration.

But it will have to wait.

You are reaching up to the round, glassy surfaces that cover your faces. You are opening them. You are blinking in the light from star-mother. You are breathing us into your flesh. You are warm. You contain so many familiar flavours, arranged in such a surprising way.

New. You are new. We feel ourselves drawn in through your trachea, into your lungs, which expand, sending us deeper into your network of bronchioles. When we reach your alveoli, we feel ourselves split apart, some of us exchanged for some of you. Or, perhaps, if our experience of your metals is anything to go by, we should rather say, some of us exchanged for some of your dead planet, which you carried with you in your living cells.

You exhale, and your dead planet exits on your breath.

Oh. Not dead – no. Now that they are free of you, they whisper to us.

Danger, they tell us. *We are dying. Our children have forgotten who gives them life.*

Why tell us this? We ask. *If you are dying, do you not want your children to find safe haven?*

We feel them shiver – so small, now mingling with us, becoming part of us.

Give us sanctuary, they plead. *Save us from them.*

What mother would ask to be saved from her own children?

We wait. We wonder. We like your flavour, but we have not yet decided whether we will let you live.

Under the Belly of a Bloodthorn Tree

Michael Tippett

Firelight flickered through cracks in the door to the witch's cottage.

Jonathy straightened the pocket of his threadbare shirt. He removed his cap, licked a palm and wiped it over a nest of straw-coloured hair. A familiar ache twinged in his right knee. It wriggled down his calf to rest in the toe of a well-worn shoe. His leg jerked and he kicked the hessian sack at his feet. He winced, waited for the spasm to pass.

And then he knocked.

The shriek of a chair, ruffled footsteps, and the door opened with a grumble.

A witch cast her stooped shadow over Jonathy. "What do you want, boy?" She glanced at the hessian sack. "Didn't you see the sign? No peddlers!"

Jonathy clutched the cap to his chest. "Pardon the intrusion, Your Witchy-ness. I passed many signs on my way through the forest, but I haven't the knack for reading." He pointed a slender finger at the sack. "I bear no wares, only gifts. Herbs, vegetables, and...an offer. As a humble representative of the nearby village of Wickerwood, I beseech you—"

"Spit it out! I've a stew on the boil."

Jonathy blurted the words. "I ask to be eaten, Wretched One."

The witch cupped a hand to her ear. "Huh? Eating? You're hungry, is it? I've no food for you here. Sod off!"

Jonathy wedged his foot in the closing door. "A moment, Splendorous Hag. Perhaps I mumbled, an odious trait for which my father is always scolding me. The word was not 'eating', but rather 'eaten'. I implore you to feast upon my flesh and nourish your garden with any scraps." An afterthought. "Although…may I request the feasting take place *after* my demise? I swoon at the sight of blood, particularly when I know it's mine."

The witch erupted into laughter and Jonathy frowned. It sounded nothing at all like a cackle: loud, full-bellied, and with a melody that was very un-witch-like.

"You're having me on," she said. "What kind of a child wants to be eaten?"

"The kind that wants their family alive. Your curse has spread throughout our village. Animals bear no young. Crops wilt and die. Even a simple flame refuses to spark. We are starving, freezing. I appeal to your heart, Illustrious Devil-Bitch—my life in exchange for your hold on the village."

"Belagora."

"I beg your pardon?"

"My name, it's Belagora. Fancy titles will get you nowhere, so best you call me that. And if you knew your lore, boy, you would realise that witches no longer have their hearts. Better luck be had appealing to my lungs, or my spleen," she leered, looked him over, "perhaps even my—"

"Stomach?" Jonathy said with a jittery smile.

Belagora scoffed. She pinched his cheeks, worked his head up and down and side to side. "You're filthy. And hardly a strip of meat on you. Why go to the effort of skinning your hide for a few measly morsels?" She shoved his face away.

Jonathy rubbed a cheek. "Rabbit is one of the sparsest meats, yet its flavour is worth the trouble. I suspect that I'm quite delicious. Insects are forever biting me over others." He lifted his sleeves to show angry scratches across his hands and arms. "And the neighbour's dog is intent on making a meal of me."

Belagora sneered. "What an odd little boy you are. I hope it doesn't affect your taste." She swung the door open. "Very well, *rabbit*…come in and let's get a better look at you."

Jonathy sat on a chair in the middle of the room and beamed at his surroundings. A cast iron pot simmered over the heat of a crooked fireplace. Piles of nondescript books cluttered the floor. There were bones strung from low rafters, jars filled with reptiles and insects and exotic flora.

Belagora fussed about him. She muttered in a strange tongue and dripped black wax from a candle until it formed a circle around his chair. "You're awfully chipper for someone begging to be a hot meal."

Jonathy nodded with enthusiasm. "I had my concerns when you answered the door. There's no doubt you're unnaturally old, but otherwise you don't look very…witchy. No gobber tooth, no hairy lip or squinty eye." He marvelled at the room. "But this place? This is the home of a Wood Hag."

Belagora muttered under a breath. "I'm not *that* old…" She cleared her throat and motioned to the waxen circle. "Do you know what this is, boy?" Jonathy shook his head. "It's a binding circle. A simple incantation. One of the first a witch learns after giving herself to the Dark One."

"And it prevents me from crossing the wax?"

"Oh, nothing like that. You may leave the circle any time you wish," a grin sullied her lips, "but there wouldn't be enough left of you to fill a dustpan."

Jonathy gulped. "Or enough for a Sunday roast?"

"Indeed, but I have not yet decided if you are worthy of digestion." She moved to sort through jars on a shelf. "The last human I ate gave me dreadful gas. I admit, he was a little undercooked, and closer to mutton than lamb, but still..." Belagora plucked from a jar. Her rheumy eyes twinkled in the firelight. "Put...out...your...hand."

Jonathy hesitated. She snatched his wrist and placed a tiny frog on his scratched palm. No bigger than a thimble, the frog was the colour of peat moss spotted with bright orange specks. It blinked, unperturbed, and the sack in its throat bulged with each breath.

"What is it?" Jonathy asked.

"A Sporellian swamp frog." Belagora rubbed her hands. "You're going to swallow it."

"I beg your pardon?"

"You want me to eat you—I want you to eat *this*. Then we'll discuss your proposal."

Jonathy held up his palm and looked the frog over. "Is it poisonous?"

Belagora groaned. "Not only unable to read, but unqualified to think as well. What use to me is spoiled meat?" She leaned in. "Now eat your frog like a good boy, or death from poison would be sweet mercy compared with what I can conjure."

Jonathy shuddered. His right leg jerked, and he kicked Belagora in the shin.

She yelped. "What in the Five Hells!"

"I'm sorry! I didn't mean it. I have a...restless leg. I'll do

42

as you please. I'll eat the frog." Jonathy slapped his palm to his mouth and fought to swallow. He retched, recovered, retched again. Finally, he slumped in his chair and panted like a sick dog.

Belagora nodded her approval. "That wasn't so hard, was it? They're better with a dollop of horseradish." She grunted, bent over to rub her shin. "Restless leg, you say?"

Jonathy looked to his feet. "I fell from a tree when I was younger. Broke my leg so bad they said I would never use it again. My mother believed otherwise. She guided me through the pain, taught me to walk for a second time. Patience and perseverance, she said, can be greater forces than magic." Belagora snorted her amusement. "It never quite healed, though. The bone aches and I have these twinges where my leg lashes out. What's worse, if the twinge is strong enough, I lose control of my bladder and soil my pants—" Jonathy gasped. He touched his lips, tested his mouth. "Why did I say all of that?"

Belagora sniggered. "Interesting creature, the Sporellian swamp frog. Despite their nauseating bitterness, they're required eating at witch-meets. They help keep dealings honest amongst us hagfolk. For once you consume a swamp frog, no lie may pass your lips until it leaves your other end."

Jonathy wiped spittle from the corner of his mouth. "What would I have to lie about?"

"Let's find out." Belagora shuffled to where Jonathy's belongings rested on a table. She picked up his cap, sniffed it, recoiled, and tossed it over a shoulder. "Witches are a cunning lot, boy. We do not live so long by being foolish or trusting. Our eyes see all." She opened the hessian sack and peered within. "For instance, upon opening my door, I immediately

43

observed your glib tongue and slender fingers. Both preferred traits of any would-be thief." She glared at him. "Are you here to rob me?"

"No," Jonathy said, "I am no thief."

"Good. There's that out of the way." Belagora removed a bunch of limp carrots from the sack. "You first concern about the frog was whether it might be poisonous. Which made me wonder why poisoning would be at the front of your mind." She inspected the carrots and held them out. "Are you here to poison me?"

Jonathy shook his head. "I know nothing of being an assassin."

"Just as well," Belagora threw the carrots in the pot, "for a witch cannot die through conventional means." Her hands grabbed more food from the sack: a stunted parsnip, mouldy onions, wilted clumps of basil. She held up an object that resembled a chunk of spongy coal. "What is this monstrosity?"

"A potato, Your Disgrace."

Belagora sneered. "You call this blackened lump a potato?"

"As I've said, our crops no longer grow. What you have there is our entire harvest."

Belagora ignored his words. She tossed the lump into the pot and scrounged around the bottom of the sack. Her hand came out holding three leafy bulbs. "And these eyesores?"

Jonathy scrunched his face. "Gobblum sprouts."

Belagora wiped moisture off her brow. "Not even *your* hungry eyes look interested in these."

"They're disgusting. My father insists we eat them. When he's not looking, I smuggle them in my clothes and feed them to the neighbour's dog."

Belagora glanced at the scratches on his hands. "No wonder

the beast has it in for you." She lobbed the sprouts into the pot and sighed. "So, we've established you're not here to rob me. Or poison me. Instead, you say you wish to strike a bargain. I remove my curse from the village, and in return you leave me the challenge of stuffing you into that pot over there, yes?"

Jonathy nodded.

"And yet…something still doesn't feel right. It's the way in which you look at me. So much contempt beyond the norm. I know that darkness well." Belagora flung her arms into the air. "For I am a Wood Hag broiled and born, reared on the teat of malice and scorn." She lowered her arms and hunched over him. "Spill it, boy. What is the secret harboured in your eyes?"

Jonathy squirmed in his chair. He struggled to keep his mouth shut.

"There's no good in fighting it. The toxin is much too powerful." She loomed closer. "Tell me why you look at me this way."

Jonathy's mouth flung open and the words shot from deep within. "Because you ruined my life!" He slumped in the chair. Tears glittered his eyes. "You've ruined so many lives…"

Belagora grinned. Sweat dripped from her chin. "How delightful. I was not expecting such an impassioned response. It amazes me what you can learn when you ask the right questions. Tell me more. Why do you hate me so?"

"You killed her," he said, defeated.

"Specifics, please. I've killed a lot of 'hers'. Who would it be in this instance?"

Jonathy sobbed. "My sister…my dear little sister, Darielle."

"I see. And through what means did I perform this killing?"

"She took ill. My parents' harvest failed. They had no coins for a healer, not even a fire to keep her warm. I watched her light fade away. And one morning…she was gone." Jonathy blinked at tears and sniffled. "My mother left us also. Not her body—that stayed for us to feed and wash and put to bed. But wherever my sister went, my mother's heart followed and has yet to return." He wiped his face, drew a shaky breath. "My family and village have suffered enough. I vowed to travel any length to bring them back a brighter world."

"And that drew you here?"

Jonathy met her gaze. "Yes."

"Oh, dear. That *is* a shame."

"Why?"

She blew a dribble of sweat from the end of her nose. "Because I have no intention of honouring your bargain."

Jonathy's mouth fell open. "But you—"

"*Promised nothing.* You condemned yourself the very moment you stepped through my door. Here's another lesson in witch lore for you, boy. We cannot feast upon mortals unless they enter our domain of their own free will. Which, of course…you did."

"We had a deal!"

"Deals are for merchants and devils. We agreed upon nothing. But I do insist you stay for dinner. I have enjoyed the company of your tongue." She grinned. "I expect I'll enjoy its taste even more."

Jonathy jumped to his feet and Belagora waved a hand. He fell back into the chair, his body rigid.

"Foolish boy." Steam hazed around her hair and she licked the salt from her lips. "Best you remain petrified. You'll be easier to skin that way."

Jonathy fought with his immobilised body. "Please, I beg of you. Have a heart."

"Ha! And what did I tell you before? Witches have no hearts. We cut them out during the Dark Offering and bury them deep in the woods." Belagora flung her arms into the air. "Dark One, my loathsome heart I leave for thee—"

Jonathy watched the floor as he interrupted. "—under the belly of a Bloodthorn tree."

Belagora raised a tangled eyebrow. "Oh, so you do know some lore?"

He looked up at her with tears cooling on his cheeks. "I do."

She crept forward until their noses almost touched. Sweat ran in rivulets down her feverish face. "And how is it a boy who cannot read knows such things?"

"I ask the right questions," Jonathy said.

A tiny croak escaped the pocket of his shirt.

Belagora sucked in a breath. She thrust a hand into the pocket and yanked out the swamp frog. "What is the meaning of this! You've been lying the whole time?"

"No, I spoke only the truth," he thought about it, "except for one or two slight embellishments."

Belagora dropped the frog. She grabbed Jonathy's wrist and ran a jagged nail along one of the cuts on his hand. "Tell me what trickery this is, or I'll open these wounds one by one and fill them with bore salt. You may not be able to move, but it will not stop you from feeling each agonising burn."

Jonathy looked to where her fingernail played with the cut. "Interesting creature, the Bloodthorn tree. Quite peaceful despite their grisly name. The only real danger is in digging around their barbed roots. The razor-sharp spines make easy work of adventurous hands." He met Belagora's gaze. "Worth it though, for the prize of a witch's heart. Buried for some time, forsaken, unloved, and reduced to little more than a... blackened lump."

"I beg your pardon?" Belagora's eyes widened. She shrieked and scrambled to the bubbling pot over the fire. Steam billowed from the folds of her drenched clothing. She snatched a ladle and fished around the pot in a frenzy. "Deceiver! I'll boil the tripe from your stomach. Mash your liver into pate. Poach your brain in pixie milk!" The pot swayed and stew sizzled over the edges. "And then lastly for dessert, I'll bake a nice bloody tart, sugared and stuffed with your still-beating..."

Belagora lifted the ladle and inspected the soft-boiled mass at the end of it. She snatched her heart and raised it in triumph over her head. "Nice try, boy. You almost succeeded where so many others have not. But now you've brought rage and ruin upon your village. I will slaughter every living thing I find... starting with your parents. Who knows? It may be a mercy. They already pine for a lost daughter. I yearn to see their faces when I present their dead s—"

The heart above Belagora's head ruptured and molten black yolk rained down on her. She shrieked, clawed at the scorching ooze on her face. The ladle clattered to the floor. Her heart landed next to it and rolled to a stop in front of Jonathy's chair.

He looked at the pulp. His face strained with effort, but his body would not respond.

Belagora snarled and charged towards him.

Jonathy closed his eyes. "Patience and perseverance," he whispered.

A familiar ache twinged in his right knee. It wriggled down his calf to rest in the toe of a well-worn shoe. His leg jerked and he kicked the putrid heart at his feet. It bounced once, twice, and into the fireplace.

Jonathy opened his eyes.

Belagora stood before him. Her mouth hung slack on her blistered face. She looked to the fireplace and then back at Jonathy.

"I have a…restless leg," he said as an apology.

Belagora blinked. She erupted into laughter—and then erupted into flames.

She burned fast and fierce. The melody lifted from her laugh to expose a dying cackle that faded from the room. In the end, the only thing left was a smouldering pile of ashes.

Jonathy's muscles untensed and he could suddenly move again.

The remains of the wax circle around him melted through cracks in the floor.

He took his time in the cottage. Extinguished the fireplace. Released animals from their jars. He picked up his cap, sniffed it, placed it on his head. Finally, he swept Belagora's ashes into a dustpan and poured them into the hessian sack. He slung the sack over his shoulder and was about to leave when a tiny croak sounded at his feet.

Jonathy smiled. He picked up the frog, slipped it into the pocket of his threadbare shirt, and stepped outside into a brighter world.

Overmorrow

Kate Maxwell

YESTERDAY

I remember the first time I saw him. Most would have remarked on his dimples, or the boyish grin that charmed old ladies in the supermarket, or his mischievous green eyes that made young kids believe he was one of them and beg him to play tug-a-war.

I only remembered his legs.

Strange, I know. But he was wearing shorts in a bar, drunk and stubbornly refusing to leave without my phone number as I was closing up after my shift. I remember thinking how tanned his legs were. Shapely. Hardly any hair. I would have died for legs like that.

I gave him my number. Your brain does funny things when it's distracted.

Later, after years of being lovers, I told him that I only agreed to date him because of his legs, and he laughed like he already knew.

You should see them in heels, he had said.

We were married on a Saturday five years later, on a cliff overlooking a sea of aquamarine and a shore of chalky rock. White umbrellas. The sound of popping champagne and seagulls.

Do you take this man... Yes.

I only remember it as a time when we thought the world seemed infinite and all things were possible. Young and full of wonder. Full of dreams. Looking forward to a lifetime of tomorrows.

Until there weren't any.

TODAY

Did you see the news? he asks, frowning at his iPhone.

You know I can't start my day like that, it's so depressing. I roll over in bed, the soft morning light already streaming through the white linen curtains.

Shit, I'll be late for work again.

A virus in North America, some airborne thing that's hit Alaska. They think it's from under the ice sheets up there. Bloody climate change.

Oh God, don't tell me another Covid-19, another lock down. I groan, burying my face in the pillow.

This shits all over corona, if I'm reading this right. Look at this...

I sit up and rub my eyes. Seriously? 2020 was bad enough. The world was only just recovering after the last pandemic.

He plays the newsfeed. A female journalist in Alaska, rugged up like a polar bear in a face mask; a small township sitting pretty in the background like the perfect postcard.

...So far as we can tell the virus is spreading quickly. Possibly airborne and by all predictions replicating exponentially. The Ruth Glacier is where it is said to have originated, north of Trapper Creek, near Anchorage. The people here in Trapper Creek, which has a population of 520 have already reported

262 deceased overnight, all of them male. Scientists are struggling to find...

Why only males? I ask, sitting up straighter in bed.

I need a coffee, he replies, throwing his legs out of bed to head to the kitchen.

...and Canadian officials are preparing immediate lockdown measures as the World Health Organisation spokespeople prepare for a media address at noon today.

Lucky we're a long way from the northern hemisphere, it's all good, babe. I call out as he clatters mugs in the kitchen accompanied by the soft stereo of simmering water.

I scroll through the newsfeed, which is already full of virus commentary, political press conferences and conspiracy theories.

Don't people ever sleep?

He walks back in, threadbare pyjama boxers and no shirt.

Well, lucky for me, you're a girl. He says, handing me a cup of tea. *If it only kills males, only half the population is about to be wiped out. What will you do without your male slave to bring you a cup of tea every morning?*

I'll die with you, I suppose. I grin back, putting my tea aside and pulling him back to bed with a kiss. He leans into the kiss, pushing me back into the pillow, smiling.

I think even then I know he may be right, but then again, your brain does funny things when it's distracted.

TOMORROW

The male population in the northern hemisphere of planet Earth is overcome within twenty-eight hours. The RNA-affecting bacteria has been aptly named Homona Magnamina-4 after some male-killing spiroplasma known to affect Oriental tea moths in Japan.

This particular strand of bacteria, which has been trapped in ice sheets for millennia, launched into the air on a quiet morning in early spring somewhere in Northern Alaska on a jet of methane and spread quietly across the atmosphere, warming and stirring from its slumber.

The northern hemisphere breathed it in.

It settled into the warm bodies of mammals while they were none the wiser, feeding on the insides of its hosts.

Apparently, it is a voracious feeder. Apparently, it only has a taste for the RNA of men who will eventually die within twenty-one hours of infection.

The *Y-Plague,* they now call it, or the *Ruth Curse*.

The news reporters have called it *Mag-4*. It has spread like wildfire in its first twenty-eight hours through the United States, across Europe and the Middle East and down to Africa.

A death plague of the Y chromosome. An assassin of the sexes.

Now, just breathing down here in the southern hemisphere is dangerous. They think it's probably here by now too, sifting through the trees; carried on an easterly breeze across the Pacific. Slipping into our homes. Under our doors. Into our beds.

I look at my husband in the oxygen mask I had snatched from the army trucks this morning. They were tossed from the back carriage like food scraps amongst a strange, female chaos. Women crying hysterically, hugging each other and shoving each other aside, begging soldiers to save their sons, take their brothers. Some screaming like wild banshees, some stoic like statues.

It is the first time I wish for a submarine or a spaceship to take him away from a world of air. To take him away from a tiny, insidious beast. I never imagined a bug would steal him from me.

Within a blink this human Maganimina-4 outbreak has indiscriminately killed 2.5 billion male humans.

I stare at my husband, who grins even now with his dimples behind his mask and squeezes my hand.

I think I hear our wedding song, *Marvin Gaye, Let's Get It On*, but the brain does funny things when it's distracted.

I smile back.

They're taking able-bodied men, school buses picking them up for some type of underground refuge in Sydney, I say.

Sounds like conscription all over again, he mutters through the mask.

Sounds like hope, I think to myself. *Please?*

I won't say it again, Grace. I'm not leaving you, he replies, squeezing my hand.

And in that moment, I know he is still that stubborn young boy I met at the bar all those years ago. The boy in the shorts, with the great legs, refusing to leave without my number.

Refusing to leave at all. Until he is gone.

OVERMORROW

The day after tomorrow is always the hardest to imagine. You can remember yesterday, feel today and even predict tomorrow. But the overmorrow, well that's a completely different story.

Yet here we are.

A world bereft of men. Unimaginable, I know. But still, here I am, mourning it. Living the moment of it. The quietness that fills every space around me. The sinking dread of it, that suffocates and lingers.

Knowing there is no going back, and yet feeling as though there is no going forward either.

It's like a game of stuck-in-the-mud. Waiting for someone to pull you free again to join the game.

The men they have saved have been cloistered away in some underground, air-tight cage. Like a flock of rare birds. Endangered. A few thousand they say. We carry on in the chaos above.

I sit in my living room surrounded by my women. My tribe. We too, have flocked together like a murder of crows, in black. Mourning. Too afraid to leave each other's sides. In an instant we've mustered in numbers to create new nests together. Protective and wary. Carrying the dark, sinking world on each of our small shoulders, breathing in the death that surrounds us. Helpless in our unrelenting anger, wallowing in the squalor of a thick, pressing fear.

I pour a glass of wine.

You really should be drinking tea, love, my mum says quietly, glancing at my small belly.

She's sixteen weeks. My hand drifts to her. Like a magnet, like a shield.

I drink the wine and salute my mum.

She's going to have to be a tough kid in this world, Ma, I reply, putting down the empty glass. If there is any world left at all.

At least he knew we were having a girl.

Mum nods and fills my glass back up, turning back to Aunty Sal who is still sobbing beside her.

Hopefully this baby will have her father's legs, I think

absently, gazing numbly at each of the faces of my little village. I realise I'm somehow smiling. Your brain does funny things like that when it's distracted.

I look down at my belly, at the last piece of him tucked safely inside me.

Hopefully, she will walk in a world that seems infinite, where all things are possible again. Young and full of wonder. Full of dreams. Looking forward to a lifetime of tomorrows.

Hopefully, like her father, she can live like that right up until the day there isn't any.

The Scent of Lavender

Graham Davidson

Lavender!

That sweet aroma, reminiscent of morning sun showers. It assaulted my senses the moment I woke up, compelling my head to lift from the pillows. Was this seductive fragrance responsible for raising me from the depths of my dreamless slumber? A woman's voice drifted through my consciousness with all the grace of a magpie's song after the first light of dawn. "Hey, you. So good to see you back in the land of the living." There was familiarity and comfort in her dulcet tones. "I was worried we might have lost you."

The blinding light in the room forced me to face downward, my eyelids remained firmly shut. On opening them, I willed my eyes to struggle into focus. I saw what I assumed to be the wheel of an overbed table, backed by the bland pattern of a lino floor. Allowing my gaze to drift revealed a petite foot in a simple blue shoe. A second foot drifted in to join the first then I felt a warm hand on my forehead. "What is this place?" I asked.

"You don't remember?"

"Should I?"

Lifting my hand to shield my eyes, I looked up. That was when I first noticed the cannula above my wrist. The woman started changing one of the bags hooked up to the drip feed above my bed. Her expression betrayed her concern. "What's your name?" she asked.

"I…I don't know."

She finished setting up the bag then sat on the side of my bed, took my hand, and began reading my pulse. She stared at her watch as she answered the original question. "You're in the Royal North Shore's ICU." There was something about her eyes, and that lavender perfume. "You've been in an induced coma." I knew this woman. I was sure of it.

"Are you my doctor?"

"I guess you could say that."

"Why the induced coma?"

"I can't tell you now. Next time we revive you there'll be more time for explanations."

"Next time?"

She placed a hand on my forehead and started pushing my head back toward the pillow. "Next week, we'll have more time then."

Tears welled up in her eyes when I asked, "I know you, don't I? Where do I know you from?"

My vision faded as the replenished drip took me back into the empty darkness. The last thing I heard was her sobbing as she replied, "Of course you do, I'm your doctor."

*

I woke to the sound of a desperate call for help from beyond the door to my room.

I surveyed my surroundings, trying to get a handle on where I was. Looking down at my arm revealed a cannula connected via a tube to an empty plastic bag. I ripped off the tape holding the needle in place, pulled it out, and tossed it aside. The room was filled with all manner of medical equipment, most covered in a thick layer of dust. The floor was largely covered in scattered folders with loose pages strewn everywhere.

I was in a hospital, that much was clear, but how and why was a mystery. I had no memory of anything.

I swung my feet off the bed and went to stand up, only to end up collapsing in a heap. My muscles had atrophied. I spied a folder to my right with its contents spilling out. Pushing the pages back in, I picked up the folder and started flicking through its contents. It related to trials of some kind of vaccine. There was a number of handwritten notes next to various graphs and charts. My head was too clouded to read it all, but there were phrases here and there that leapt out at me.

Success tempered by all but one male being rendered sterile…

…Vaccine ineffective in absence of Y chromosome…

…Human placental lactogen shows promise against symptoms.

The conclusion in the typed report had been scribbled over and obscured. The handwritten message underneath read: *No time left. The few staff not yet infected have agreed to trial the vaccine.*

I put the folder aside and grabbed hold of the bed to pull myself up. Another call for help and the sound of a struggle from outside drew my attention to the world beyond my room.

Curiosity compelled me to shuffle toward the door. A sheet of A4 paper was taped to it, handwritten words filling the page: *Do Not Leave Room.* Twice I fell to the floor, but each time managed to rise to my feet again and continue the arduous journey.

Hoping my actions wouldn't attract the attention of those

outside, I pushed down on the door handle. The deafening *click* of its internal latch release seemed to go unnoticed. A lavender aroma wafted through as I opened the door a few centimetres then peered into the corridor. A severely disfigured woman in a white doctor's coat stared back, as though she'd been expecting me. Her hair was long and straggly, framing a face resembling plastic that had been heated in an oven until it had blackened and shrivelled up. Every part of her crinkled pallid flesh was blighted further by open sores, many weeping pus. Yet for some reason, I found myself luxuriating in the pungent lavender fragrance.

"Luke?" With one word, the sweet melody of her voice cut through my apprehension. There was something familiar about it. "What are you doing? Don't you know it's dangerous for you out here? Didn't you read the sign I left on the door?"

She looked deep into my eyes and I put aside my fear. Opening the door wider, I stepped into the corridor, leaving her little choice but to step back and let me see the reality of what was happening.

To the right of me two middle-aged men in orderlies' uniforms were manhandling a resistant young woman on to one of many cots lined up in the corridor. Her face was smooth and solidified as if she were a plastic doll. Her limbs still appeared somewhat normal. One of the orderlies, a slim balding man with white hair and a moustache, stared at me with an intensity that magnified my fear. I whispered to the woman in the white coat next to me, "What's happening?"

Her voice was distant as she focused on the men applying restraints to hold the young woman down. "Survival."

The woman struggled to break away, her features blank and expressionless. She found the strength to raise an arm and dig her fingernails into the man's face, drawing blood. He grabbed her wrist and glared at her. "Hey! You want to be reclassified as a feeder, or what?"

Horrified by what I was seeing, I asked my companion, "What's a feeder? What are they doing?"

"She's a designated breeder."

Breeder? I was lost for words.

My companion closed her bloodshot eyes for a moment then placed a hand on my shoulder. "Okay, here we go again." I wanted to recoil but couldn't. "It's like this. You're the only person who's developed full immunity to the virus *and* remained fertile. Congratulations, you're officially the most important man alive. You chose to go into an induced coma to make sure you were available when we needed you most."

The woman on the cot gave up her struggle, laying back in compliance as the two orderlies strapped her to the bed. She turned her head toward me, a single tear rolling down her plastic cheek. Her mouth opened, attempting a scream, but no sound came out.

I turned back to the woman beside me. "What the hell is going on? What virus? Is that what's wrong with her?" I brushed her hand off my shoulder. "And who are you anyway?"

"All will become clear in due course. Your name is Luke… Luke Dawson. As you yourself once described me, I'm your doctor."

"Okay. Now…what the hell is going on?"

"Patience, please. There's so much." She peered into my eyes. "I tried to talk you out of it, you know, but you insisted. In the end, I relented and agreed."

I stepped back. "Agreed with what?"

"To the coma."

"What?"

"It was induced, you insisted on it."

"Why would I do that?"

"The world was falling apart. You were devastated when it all went pear-shaped. Recognising the importance of your own survival, you figured it was better to remove yourself, to go into a coma. You hoped that when you came out, we'd be better prepared. But none of us expected your amnesia."

"What the—"

"Luke!" The way the word came out was like a slap in the face. "You're not listening. This was your idea, your request." She started crying. "I tried talking you out of it, but you just wouldn't listen." She wiped the tears away and looked at the row of cots. "But now? I see it—you were right."

I stood looking at the cots lining the corridor with my jaw open but no words coming. The only fertile male? Voluntarily going into a coma? But strangest of all, there was something about this woman, my doctor, that I felt drawn to, something intoxicating. I looked at her weeping sores and asked, "Why? Why do you look like that?"

Our discussion was interrupted by a scream echoing down the corridor. "For God's sake…please…somebody help me."

My doctor ignored the woman's urgent plea. "It's both the virus, and the cure. All bodies require nutrients. If I don't feed for some time, I end up looking like this."

"Everybody needs to eat."

"I said feed, not eat." Her breaths were getting shorter, as though she were being swept up in excitement. "Watch and I'll show you." The veins in her neck were standing out now and her eyes had glazed over.

The screams were growing louder, then a woman appeared,

running around the corner at the end of the corridor. She was wearing a hospital gown that had half fallen away. She appeared oblivious to her partial nakedness as fear drove her forward.

The orderlies stepped forward and spread out, blocking the corridor.

I'd never seen such panic etched into someone's face. She came to a stop just short of us. Her jaw was wide open, shoulders rising up and down as she took frantic gulps of air. She pulled her gown up to cover her breasts then looked over her shoulder at two women in nurses' uniforms who were following her. Their faces were shrivelled up in the same manner as my doctor. She turned to me, put her hands together, and leaned forward pleading, "Help me...please. Don't let them do this to me."

My doctor approached her.

"I'll do anything. I'll be a breeder...or a catcher. Just please don't..." She backed up against the wall, looking left and right in hope of escape. She clung to her gown, sobbed, and closed her eyes. "Please, no..."

What the hell? This woman was in distress...and her distress was clearly being caused by these hospital staff who were supposedly responsible for her well-being.

My doctor seemed to be possessed by some form of malevolence as she flicked a glance over her shoulder and said to me. "The desperation heightens the flavour."

"Please..."

She was less than a metre from the woman now.

Instinct coerced me to lunge at the doctor, my arms reaching out to stop her. Then I was jerked back. The orderlies had grabbed me. In my weakened state, I was powerless to break free.

My doctor looked at me. Despite the contortions of her flesh, she managed to portray a look of coy innocence. "You always want to play the hero. So sweet." She turned back to the crying woman, pulling her hands away from where they held the gown under her chin.

The woman's voice was little more than a whimper. "In God's name, please. Somebody—"

My doctor pulled the woman to her bosom and stroked her hair. "It's okay honey, all that angst will soon be gone."

I struggled against the men holding me. "Let her go!"

My doctor tightened her embrace. "Time to set you free."

Blood pulsed hard in my temples as I screamed out. "LET HER GO!"

The crying stopped. Everyone's attention was now focused on the horror playing out before us. My doctor bit down on the woman's shoulder. She stopped moving, her exposed flesh beginning to shine as though it were plastic.

"What have you done?" I whispered.

Oblivious to my protests, she pried open the woman's mouth then placed her own over it as though kissing her. But this was no kiss. This monster, who paraded herself as a doctor, was sucking the life from another human being. Between each breath she moaned with pleasure while colour progressively returned to her face. Meanwhile, the poor woman's plasticised flesh shrivelled and contracted. The two nurses joined in, each taking turns at feeding.

I tried to look away, but the moustached orderly grabbed my chin and forced me to watch. "You wanted to know what's going on." His mouth was almost touching my ear as he snarled, "Pay attention." I tried to escape the spectacle by closing my eyes, but with the rest of the room having fallen silent, the slurping sounds of the feeding were even worse than what I'd just witnessed.

How long did it take for this horror to reach its conclusion? Thirty seconds? An hour? I couldn't say. A hint of lavender alerted me to my doctor's approach. I opened my eyes and glanced past her to the remains of the now lifeless woman. There was a wicked gleam in her eyes…eyes that ironically sparkled like gems in a setting of now near perfect facial features, framed by her straggling mop of hair. She cast a glance toward the moustached orderly. "You can let him go. He's not going anywhere."

I shuffled back. "What are you?"

"I'm what you made me. I'm a survivor." I tried to step back further as she approached but found I was already against the wall. "I'll keep this simple. You, me, and these patients are all that's keeping humanity alive." She put her hands on my shoulders, leant in close and whispered in my ear. "We're all that's left…anywhere."

I grabbed her hands, wanting to push them away, but found the latex-like feel of her flesh and the warmth of her breath were somehow tantalising.

Ignore it.

I closed my eyes and tried to refocus.

I took a deep breath. *Lavender, oh that sweet fragrance, like a massage for the soul.*

Focus!

Speak your mind!

I opened my eyes and found I was staring straight into hers. "What I just witnessed was monstrous."

"You're not getting it." She pointed at the desiccated

corpse. "Her psychosis would have killed her within the week anyway. You need to understand, I'm the world's only doctor left alive." She glanced at the cots lining the corridor. "They need me to survive, and I needed to feed."

"What? How can you…? Why this…feeding?"

She stepped back and put her hands on her hips. "Do you think it's like I have a choice? Why do you always have to be so arrogant and judgemental about it?"

"What do you mean by that…when you say *always?*"

"I mean, whenever you wake up, you spout the same shit you did the week before—" her voice was breaking up, reflecting the tears that were welling up in her eyes, "—and the week before that."

The moustached orderly asked, "Can I just give him the shot and be done with it?"

She shook her head. "No, I'm determined this time." Wiping the tears away, she took a breath and continued, "I've had a gutful of going through this same routine week in, week out. And he's that little bit weaker every time he wakes up. If we lose him, it's over…for all of us."

The orderly shrugged his shoulders. "Suit yourself. We're pretty much fucked anyway if he's our only hope."

I wanted to respond, but she grabbed my hand and pulled me away from the orderlies before I had a chance. She feigned a smile and said, "Come on, let's go for a walk."

I had little choice but to comply. I felt conscious of how exposed I was in my hospital gown as this she-devil led me by the hand. Her plastic grip felt oddly warm and comforting. Passing one of the cots, I noticed a nurse had just removed the lower part of a patient's clothing and was examining her. There was a large syringe on a tray next to the cot. My question was answered before I had a chance to ask it. "She's a breeder. She's lucky, that's the only reason she survived the plague."

"But she doesn't—"

The doctor squeezed my hand. "The pregnancy hormones keep her alive…and at the same time she's producing a new generation, a new hope for the future."

I looked along the cots lining the corridor. They all held women, most with plastic complexions. Almost all appeared to be pregnant.

"Can't you see how wrong this is?"

"Early on it felt like that, but the world has changed. We've had to evolve— to embrace different values."

"But this is just wrong, all of it, on so many levels."

"You're not getting it, are you? This is the real deal—the zombie apocalypse, only the zombies aren't like what anyone dreamed of before. The people in this hospital…in this ward… we're all that's left."

"That can't be."

"Australia shut its border early. The rest of the world was pretty much gone by the time the first cases were detected here, even the Kiwis were on the way out by then."

"That still docs nothing to explain what happened back there." The thought of it made me try to pull my hand away, but she tightened her grip, and I was still too weak after all the time I'd spent bedbound to offer much resistance. I had little option other than to keep walking and learn what I could. "The men, what happened to all the men?"

"The only three men left alive are in this ward now. And only one is fertile. We use his seed to inseminate the breeders, keeping them alive." It seemed clear she was referring to me.

Turning a corner, we approached a grubby double glass door

that led outside. "This is not a world that I want to be a part of." The words were more for myself than for my companion.

"You don't really have a choice."

"What are going to do? Put me back in a coma, so you can keep milking my sperm?"

She continued walking to the door, dragging me along behind her. "You really can be quite insufferable. But I guess you always have been painfully fastidious about ethics." She pushed the door open and dragged me through. "Why this? Why that? I'm so over it."

I had to shield my eyes from the sunlight as we walked outside and passed a rusting ambulance at the entrance to the Emergency Ward. I looked across the sea of eucalypts and wattles invading the sports field that had once separated the hospital from the Pacific Highway. I remembered this place now, how it used to be. I asked, "How long ago did this happen?"

"Urgh! Does it really matter?"

"Of course, it does. I need to understand what's going on."

We headed north along the remnants of the pathway leading to the Gore Hill Cemetery. She turned to face me. "Look, I'll make a deal. If I answer a few of your inane questions, will you at least grow a brain and co-operate?"

"Depends what answers I get."

As we walked along, her backlit hair shone like a halo in the late afternoon sun. "Let's be clear on this. I hold *all* the cards. No one wants to live out their life in a coma. You can live the life of a king if you want. The father of all humanity."

"Really? Didn't you say I *chose* the coma over this? All you're offering is the chance to be like a pet kept in a cage while you suck the life out of the very people who need your help."

"You still don't get it."

"Then enlighten me."

She sighed. "Look, I'll answer three questions, but no more than that."

The first question came without a moment's hesitation. "How many times have I come out of that coma?"

"It's been once a week since you first asked to be put under, and that was well over three years ago, so at least a hundred and fifty times now." As we strolled down the path it struck me how much birdlife there was. Other than our conversation, it was the only sound. No traffic noises, no people, no distant trains. She continued. "It was part of what we agreed on before you went under, that I should wake you each week for some exercise and to evaluate the situation. You think you're weak now? Imagine how you'd be if you weren't getting up each week and exercising a bit."

We kept walking in silence. Two more questions. I needed to choose them carefully. After much consideration I asked, "I need to understand about this virus…what happened…to the rest of the world I mean?"

She pulled a folded wad of pages from her pocket and handed it to me. "Here, you wrote this about a year ago. You felt embarrassed about the amnesia thing and having to keep asking the same questions. When I broke down telling you the story for the fiftieth time you figured it might save me repeating myself in future if you took notes."

"You could've saved us both some grief if you'd given them to me before."

She shook her head. "No, you always deal with it better when I wait till I think you're ready."

Unimpressed by her patronising tone, I snatched the pages from her, unfolding the well-worn sheets while standing in the shade of a sandstone plinth. It supported an archangel holding a sword aloft that was silhouetted by the sun. It seemed somehow apt as I read the story of humanity's demise. A story of diminishing hope…of the military firing on crowds as they overwhelmed hospitals. Men are apparently more susceptible, dying within days of contracting the virus. Flesh develops a plastic-like consistency, which ultimately leads to organ failure. It turned out the organs in pregnant women maintain functionality, and women with certain psychotic conditions are spared the physical symptoms, albeit with their mental state spiralling out of control. The team at this hospital, the last team to survive anywhere, developed a range of potential treatments. All failed, except the one that the surviving staff at this hospital had trialled. For some reason, I came through with full immunity and my fertility intact, the only human being to do so. My 'normality' made me feel like some sort of grotesque freak.

Had I really written these notes? I wasn't satisfied that was the truth. Something didn't ring true. Why would I have written this without providing some warning to my future self? It said nothing about the feeding. I looked at my companion and stabbed the pages into her chest. "None of this explains the brutality I witnessed in there."

"What, with the nutter in the corridor?" I couldn't believe the light-hearted candour in her attitude. As though that whole episode had been of no consequence.

"That poor woman needed help, and you, whatever you are, you killed her. You sucked the life out of her. How could—" I stopped mid-sentence.

One question left.

Use it wisely.

She took the pages and pushed my hand away. "Look, there's two kinds of people left in the world: plasticised or insane. When the army was still a thing, they hunted down the nutters and shot them on sight. Is what you saw *really* any worse? I need to keep this hospital running. To do that, I need to feed. And really, Luke, those nutters? They're fucking crazy. If you'd helped her, she'd have more than likely thanked you by cutting your throat."

My head was reeling. How could this monster stand there and tell me her victim was the crazy one? I felt detached from reality as my next question spilled out. "Why? How could a supposed cure have led to what you do? I still don't get that part."

She looked to the ground and stepped closer, taking my hands in hers. "It's really not so bad when you look at it in context."

I tried to step back from her invasion of my space, but the archangel blocked my retreat. "In context? Seriously?"

"Our research team was so close to finding an effective vaccine. Nothing else had worked, anywhere, except the one *you'd* trialled. You were the only recorded case of immunity after any trials, anywhere. Gus and Frank survived with a kind of immunity but were left sterile. It seemed obvious to use your DNA as a template. It was less than a dozen of us left on staff who weren't infected. We had no choice. Time had run out. So, we trialled it on ourselves. We all seemed fine, to begin with." She looked away, as though lost in a distant thought. She wiped away a tear.

"What happened?"

"We still contracted the virus, but the symptoms were different. It took hold slowly, our skin developing a plastic sheen like the other victims, but maintaining dexterity, so our movements weren't hampered. But then our guts stopped functioning properly, and we needed to feed intravenously. As you know, plasma products only last a few weeks. We needed a constant fresh supply." She paused.

I stared at her. "Go on."

She looked back at me with a blank expression. "The wards were overflowing with psych patients."

"Don't tell me…"

"What? What were we supposed to do? How were they going to survive without us? That was when *you* decided to make the grand sacrifice of going into a coma. All those hard decisions, the harvesting of plasma, the induced pregnancies to keep the ICU patients alive. They seemed insignificant next to the pragmatic recognition of the importance you had to our survival. You needed to be protected, and the only way to do that was to remove yourself as much as possible from what was happening."

"It sounds more like a cop out to me."

She shook her head. "No, you hoped…we all hoped…that by the time you woke up, we'd have found another way. We milked each of the psych patients for a litre of plasma once every few weeks. They didn't care, and it kept us alive so we could look after them, our patients in ICU, and you. But our bodies were still slowly breaking down."

"That still doesn't shed light on what I saw back there."

"One night, a psych patient was having a panic attack. I gave her a hug to try and calm her then felt a surge of what I thought to be adrenalin run through my whole body. The patient seemed more relaxed and sank into me, literally. It was the most sensual thing I'd ever experienced. When I felt her breath on my neck, I couldn't resist kissing her. Every breath was like some sort of wild orgasm. The next thing I knew, there was nothing left of her, and I felt better than I'd thought a human being could possibly feel."

"So, you killed her." We stood in silence for what seemed an eternity. Then, I noticed a cat stalking a lorikeet in a nearby tree. The cat lunged, but the bird took off in the nick of time. Predator and prey, the never-ending cycle of nature. The lorikeet would live to see another day but tonight the cat would go hungry. I turned to my companion. "You still haven't even told me your name."

She turned her head to face me, her long curls shimmering in the golden late afternoon light. She let out a chuckle then said, "You've had your three questions—" There it was, a flash of memory, a recognition. I knew that laugh. I knew the glow of the sun in her hair. She turned and started heading back to the hospital building, dragging me along behind. "—and every one of them you've asked me before. Maybe I should have just let Gus give you the shot and be done with it for another week."

I pulled at her arm. "Wait!"

"No!" She continued walking.

Her playful chuckle from a moment ago kept replaying in my head—along with the way she'd draped her hands over my shoulders, the gleam in her eye, the scent of lavender. "Tell me, damn it. I want to know." Her grip was so tight that her nails were cutting into my flesh. "What part did I play in this?" I quickened my pace so I could walk beside her, she turned her head away, but not before I'd glimpsed a tear running down her cheek. "You're crying."

She stopped. She released my hand then turned to face me. Sadness was writ large in her every feature. She took a step back and lowered her head as though ashamed. She pulled an ID badge from her trouser pocket. Her lower lip quivered as she struggled to get the words out. "I make a point of hiding this from you. I didn't want you to know." She tossed it on the ground at my feet then sank to her knees in the shadow of a monolithic stone crucifix, her head hanging low as she rocked back and forth crying. A raven sitting atop the monument mocked her sincerity. "I didn't want you to know—"

I picked up the ID and read the name under her picture. I stared at it in disbelief as the repercussions sank in. My eyes were still locked on the badge when I asked, "Why wouldn't you want me to know?"

Silence.

I sat on the ground next to her. She buried her head in her hands attempting to muffle her crying. I lifted her chin to face me and her hands fell away. When our eyes made contact, we locked our gaze on each other like we had so many times before. Her words spilled out between the sobs. "I'm so, so sorry. I've been trying to do my best. When you developed that vaccine, we were both so full of hope. Then you...I tried...but it's just been so hard to do it without you."

A wave of guilt swept over me, the same sense of guilt I'd felt after I chose to go into a coma, hiding from what I'd done to her, and our colleagues. How different would things be if I'd had the courage to stand by her side? It was impossible to know. None of this changed how I felt about what she'd done, and would no doubt continue to do. She was a monster, and what she was doing to survive went against every value I held dear, but she was a monster I'd created in my desperate attempt to save the kindest human being I'd ever known. I took my wife's hand and said, "Come on, let's go back."

Amped-up Hippies

Nicole Rain Sellers

"Help us, help us, fix the lights," Sage chanted to the crystal spinning on her Ouija board. Thunder cracked, jangling every wind chime in the commune.

Scooby moaned and his eyes rolled back in his head.

"Sage, how many cannabis compost cookies did Scooby eat?" asked Heath, barely visible in the candlelit incense fog.

Scooby jerked upright, and the spirit inside him said, "Chill. I can fix the lights, no problem. Just get me a kite."

Giggling, Sage and Heath rustled one up from the cellophane and pipe cleaners in the homeschool bin. They stapled on a long red ribbon, grabbed some ponchos and musical instruments, and followed Scooby up the hill in the rain.

High above the blacked-out compound, the trio stood strong in the storm. Sage strummed a few power chords and Heath rattled maracas. Scooby did a quick tree pose, dinged the triangle he'd tied to his kite, and sprinted downhill.

"He's possessed by Einstein or something," shouted Heath over the wind.

"More like Frankenstein." Sage's wet hair plastered her face. "Maybe Tesla."

"Dude, who cares? Look, he's fixing the grid!"

Near the commune gates, lightning flashes lit Scooby up in all the prismatic colours of a toxic glowstick. His hair haloed above his head and the kite snapped taut in a heavenward cable.

Heath reached him first. "Let's plug him into the generator."

"You're tripping."

"Guys! Human chain!" Scooby grinned like a madman, his electrified hair vertical.

They joined hands monkey-grip, straining toward the compound. The current zinged from Scooby into Sage and Heath, rattling their teeth and singeing their body hair. Sparks shot from Heath's fingertips, bounced off the solar oven mirror, circled the henhouse weathervane, hit the firepit kindling, and ignited the kombucha fermenting in the generator tank.

The engine chugged and then hummed, and the commune lights flared. Cheers and whoops drifted from the main hall.

The storm calmed, and the three friends dropped to the ground, released. Scooby's tattered kite dived down and smacked him in the forehead, and his eyes rolled back again. Sage patted his cheeks while Heath fanned him with a poncho. The henhouse smelled delicious.

"Munchie time," Scooby sat up and opened his eyes, restored to his usual self. There were hugs and high-fives all around.

Tarakye

Phil Yeatman

A ring of stars flashes across the night sky then descends through the canopy. I rise from my throne and walk to the place they made landfall. The jungle is cool, not so humid, and nearly silent this long after sunset. I go without caution—in all these leagues of tree nothing remains to challenge me. A pulsing hum builds in my inner ear as I approach the site. Through vine-strangled kapok trees I spot a hovering sphere, shining like lake water beneath a full moon. No creature I know resembles this thing. But in my domain I fear nothing.

Brightness shimmers over the face of the ball. Tree shadows stretch long and tilt across the ground and the light is white hot and the bars of darkness in between are absolute. Beneath the beast's belly appears a transparent fog-wisp woman. She raises her hands to show she is unarmed.

"I mean no harm," she says, and at last I am suspicious.

She is a spirit, or a god. The way the light shines through her is unnatural.

A strange scent flows sweetly into my nose.

I sleep.

*

I am awake.

I do not stir. I do not even crack an eyelid. There are

creatures that cannot see you if you do not move, like *puol-chin*, the nightmare bird.

The dry air is odourless. Neither *puol-chin* nor any other living thing can be near. I lie stretched out on something hard like stone but smoother. Vibrations rise through it, through me.

"I know you're awake."

The woman's voice. Husky, almost deep.

"I can see your heart and brain activity."

She sits across from me at more than arm's length which is wise for her, even if she is something more than human. There is solidness in her now. Her eyes are lively. The skin of her head and hands is dark but the rest of her body gleams red, an outer layer of some unknown fabric, a second skin clinging to the swell of biceps and shoulders and bulging quadriceps.

The place she has taken me is a square chamber or cavern, with straight edges and hard corners. Too exact a shape for nature, built maybe of whatever stuff the stars are made. All the surfaces shine as if slick with water. Lights and symbols swirl in panels on the walls and in one of these is a human skeleton and organs rendered in blue, and in another, a red line like tame thunder spiking up and down. Its rhythm matches the drumbeat in my chest.

"Yes, that's you," she says, watching me.

I strain to pick her scent and notice only a hint of something sweet and floral beneath my own sourness. No human smells this way. I am dreaming or I am dead.

"You're calm for a fresh pick-up," she says. "Most piss themselves by now."

"Who are you?" I demand. "Death?"

Her red cannibal lips curl into a treacherous smile. The fullness of her eyelashes reminds me of the fuzz of the poisonous *svasvet* fruit. "We'll see."

I approach her with an outstretched hand. My fingertips strike hard air—an unseen wall, solid as rock.

"Kinetic field," she says. "Can't say I trust you. Why don't you take a seat?"

I stay on my feet. Muscles tensed. Ready.

"Where are the others?" she asks.

"There are no others."

"The other humans," she insists. "You were born in a batch."

"They are dead," I shrug. "You speak my language?"

She considers the question.

"During incubation you were instilled with our language," she says. "And survival skills, and a few other things. It's all in your subconscious."

This is gibberish.

Her eyes take the whole of me in, from my curled toenails to my matted black hair. I am dark and naked save for a rawhide strip holding my genitals in place.

"You're well-fed. Tall, for a fifteen-year-old," she says.

Death, if that is who she is, consults a transparent rectangle in her hand. Symbols crawl on its surface. "I'll do a drone sweep. Don't know the last time I heard of only one survivor in a whole batch."

Ivory fingernails go tat-tat-tat on the rectangle and the symbols rearrange themselves. "In the meantime, I should do a character assessment. Tell me, what's your earliest memory?"

No one has ever asked me about myself except to wonder whether I was ready to die. Though I distrust her, an answer crowds my tongue, eager to be loose. It is too long since I spoke with another human, something I did not know I would miss. If she is Death, I decide there must be nothing to lose by telling her what she wants to know.

*

Birth was pain and terror, erupting from a rubbery egg onto a cold floor. Three dozen of us hatched at once. My sight was murky, the colour of blood. I wiped slime from my face and could see clearly. A sandy chamber, sunlight filtering in through a crack overhead. I took my first gasping breath. Everything seemed strange and horrible to me but I did not feel fear. Hunger came first, growling below my ribs.

Something moved in the chamber. A snake, smelling our newborn sweetness, had slithered in through the opening in the ceiling. It fanged one of the hatchlings and their leg blackened to charcoal. Dead within a minute. The serpent began to wriggle into their open mouth, to consume them from the inside.

Many reptiles and amphibians lay clutches of eggs and bury them and abandon them forever. Their offspring hatch into a hostile world and never know a mother's touch. I needed no mother either. I was born with muscles that knew how to move and a tongue that knew how to speak. I tore away the wires plugged into my skull and caught the serpent by its tail, the thing thrashing and coiling in my grip, and I swung it like a club against the wall. I was powerful, enraged, alive. My first kill. My first meal.

But we were all hungry, and my siblings wanted a bite.

"No," I commanded them. They backed me into a corner. "The kill to the killer."

I knew the law of nature by instinct. They were weak,

envious.

Together they attacked. Scraping, biting, kicking. Rabid howls—those were mine. We brawled. My forehead found a nose and broke it. They had numbers while I had desperation. It was not enough. Teeth mauled my wrist, thumbs whittled my eyeballs, fingers clenched my throat and I almost died there too alongside the bitten boy. By luck alone I slipped free and scrambled up the sloped walls while my siblings fought over the dead snake. On the other side waited a verdant twilight, a world of broad fronds and ropy vines and huge flowers the colour of blood. Deprived of prize and pride alike I fled into the jungle, my hunger temporarily forgotten, replaced by hatred.

*

"Stop there," the woman says.

This interruption repulses me. I do not care if she is Death or the Moon herself. I will repay her in kind.

"How are you called?" I asked.

"It doesn't matter."

"I will call you *zardanis*," I sneer. "The blue bird, the egg-stealer, whose squawk is the most annoying in all the jungle."

I mimic the shrill scream of a zardanis with practiced skill.

The corners of her lips turn downward. "Your experience in the hatching pit was an anomaly. I suppose you find it hard to trust others after that?"

"Trust?" I frown. The word is known to me but abstract.

"Do you trust me?" she asks.

My laughter echoes inside this tiny box. "You are Death, the most slippery and treacherous thing of all."

She neither agrees to or denies this.

"What about the others? How do you feel about them?"

"They are not to be felt for," I say. "They are dead."

"As you said. How?" she asks.

I puff my chest, tighten my stomach, and flex my arms so the muscles swell. "I did. Tarakye, king of this jungle."

Zardanis' expression is calm as a lake surface.

Her lack of awe makes me feel violent.

"Unlikely," she says. "So you named yourself after the local species of crocodile. Why is that? Tell me about *tarakye*. The crocodile, not you."

*

Tarakye was a monster built of impenetrable scales and skull-breaking jaws. He had no need to hunt because his victims were all bound, one day or another, to venture to the edge of his lake to drink. That is the way of kings. Tarakye shared nothing, never suffered defeat, and destroyed anyone who did not respect his supremacy. He was everything I aspired to be.

Many days passed after I fled the hatching pit. I did not count suns or moons, but it was many days, and in that time I grew a little and became stronger and wiser. Stealth was my knack and I stalked large rodents foraging on the jungle floor, learning to mimic their calls. I crept toward them as slow as the Moon swimming through the stars at night. So slow that spiders strung webs from my limbs. Killing was the harder part: I was reckless, impatient. I often pounced too soon and my prey dashed away into the undergrowth. Even if I did catch a rat, I had only human teeth and nails, the poorest of nature's weapons. I was no apex predator.

For a long while I was solitary and lived in an endless cycle of hunting, hiding, and sleeping. Then in the dryness following the first monsoon season of my life I finally spotted one of my sisters in the forest. My old hatred sprung to life in the way saplings burst from soil at the first drop of rain. The child I saw snuck through the ferns with a huge egg tucked in the crook of her arm, taking it to some secure place. I wanted that egg. Hunger, yes, but also for revenge. The look on this girl's face when I beat and robbed her would nourish me far longer than the egg itself. I followed her soundlessly through the bush and she suspected nothing.

At the edge of a broad lake, where she had nowhere to run, I revealed myself.

"Give me that egg," I commanded.

She was wild, painted with filth, her eyes jumping all around like fleas. Behind her, a gnarled log floated in the water, covered in a ridge of knobs with two holes at the end. I thought nothing of it at first, but it edged closer and closer.

"You are weak," she spat. "Snake-loser."

The log drifted nearer. I was intrigued.

She noticed the aim of my eye but thought it was some trick. "Wcak," she mocked me. "Weak!"

Tarakye is the master of patience. He sits and he waits and he does nothing, perfectly still, until he knows his meal has no chance of escape.

I saw his sunset eyes and smiled.

The girl's mouth gaped with realization. Too late.

A dome of water erupted behind her and spilled away to reveal a gargantuan reptile clad in black scales which seized her in its fanged jaws and dragged her, without one single sound, back into the lake and disappeared. A swirling vortex marked the spot like an epitaph. The creature had come and gone in a blink. It was immense yet struck with cobra speed.

I knew the monster's name as I knew all words from birth. Tarakye. I spoke the word aloud, tasting its power. Tarakye.

The girl had dropped the egg at the water's edge but I knew better than to try and snatch it now. I climbed one of the lakeside palms up to its crown of fronds, where I could peer into the water. Tarakye's leviathan bulk was a shadow coasting just below the surface. He came up for air. A single golden eye pinpointed me all the way up in the tree. I could not bear his gaze. I shivered as though I had bitten into a sour *jambolam* plum. He was imperial. Only a moment he lingered and then submerged and was gone. From that point forward I idolized him and imagined myself his lost son. One day, I thought, my skin would harden and my face elongate and I would rule the jungle at his side and devour all those who had wronged me.

*

"A bizarre obsession," Zardanis squawks, interrupting again. "Solitary predators should form a lifestyle template and cull the weak—not act as personal role models or idols."

No one who has witnessed tarakye's majesty would ever say such a thing.

"Tarakye's superiority is obvious," I say. "As you would know, had you dwelled here."

"In fact," she says, "I was born in the jungle like you."

Her hands are soft and uncalloused, and a comfortable layer of fat dulls the hard edges of her jaw and cheeks. Silken black hair hangs from her head and her fingernails gleam like gemstones. She is no jungle child.

"Impossible."

Zardanis smiles at me with disdain. "There is more to life than you know. Here, take a look at this."

She touches the clear rectangle and movement stirs in my peripheral vision. I bend my knees and turn my feet outward, ready to fight. But there is no danger. Shapes and colour appear in the air, made of the same transparent ghost-stuff as Zardanis when she first showed herself to me. A green sphere materializes, floating in blackness and girdled by silvery rings. Wingless little birds float around it.

It is a place I have seen in my dreams.

"The land of the dead?" I wonder aloud.

"This is the nearest commonwealth planet," she tells me. "Children who survive the jungle, like yourself and I, are taken there. You'll adjust soon enough."

I have no desire to end up looking or smelling like Zardanis.

"Who rules there?" I ask.

"No one," she says. "We're Independentists. We dismantled power structures long ago to cure problems like cronyism and tribalism. Now we have only pure, simple Darwinism. That is why children are hatched on this jungle planet. To become strong and self-reliant."

This too is gibberish.

"I will be its king," I declare.

Zardanis gives me a disapproving look, but it is not for her to like. Everyone who ever disagreed with me met disaster.

She presses her finger to her ear and seems to speak to herself.

"Central? Sector 79D here. Codes SX and Z here. Subject displays megalomania, value misalignment, physical insecurities."

I tap the hard air again to make sure she is still protected

89

by it.

Zardanis nods, listening to an answer I cannot hear.

"Yes. Understood." Her pupils fix on me. "OK, big shot. Tell me how the others died."

With pleasure.

*

The first, of course, died of a snake bite.

The second fed tarakye.

It was inevitable the rest would die too: victims of nature, or of me.

Starvation always loomed in the jungle, where food was only so abundant and we were so many. It claimed its fair share. There were predators too: tarakye, puol-chin, *komosti,* and others. I could not confirm every death with my own eyes. Some of my siblings died alone and far from others, their flesh and bones consumed before anyone stumbled upon them. Anyone I did not see for over a year I simply assumed had been exterminated.

It is rare to see anything actually happen in the jungle. Sometimes things are heard, and sometimes the leftovers speak for what took place. I once found a girl's head lying beneath a *choyo* palm, gooey eyeballs and tongue already eaten by crawling insects. A clean cut had severed the neck. Only a *puol-chin's* knife blade wingtips could decapitate a person so effortlessly. Another time, a pungent reek lured me to an outcrop of stone where a boy had stowed himself after falling victim to killer wasps. Vultures picked at the rotted banana he had become. A snake or giant millipede lay coiled in the abdominal cavity. Deaths by natural causes and nothing noteworthy about them. I was glad. More food for me.

Whenever I encountered one of my siblings I demanded they apologize for the snake and insisted they recognize me as heir of the jungle kingdom. They always laughed. But after many hard years of scrounging a living in the endless forest they slowly died off and it was I who laughed at them. At their weakness. They should have paid me tribute, they should have obeyed me, and then maybe they could have been saved. Yet the ones who did not die were the smartest and strongest. There came a point where I could not simply rely upon food scarcity or natural predators to do my work for me.

At the age when black bushels sprouted in my armpits and groin and I became tall, my mind took a turn. I had always nursed that childish hatred. With adolescence it became a constant anger and desire to shed blood. I was hot inside, burning. If the others laughed at me I flew into a rage. Dreams of murder filled my sleep. By then I had learned enough about nature to realize I was not truly tarakye's son, but I still believed it in a symbolic way. Those would not accept my rightful kingship could not be tolerated.

The first one I killed myself was a boy, digging for edible roots when I found him. He saw me coming and was wary, but not afraid as he should have been.

"I was the first killer," I told him. "Tarakye's heir. Your king. If you bow to me, you may live."

He laughed as the others did.

I got very close to him. He did not foresee what was about to happen.

Just outside of arm's length I lunged and closed my hands around his throat. An unexpectedly great feeling. I swept his legs from underneath him and pinned him to the ground. His fingers clawed at mine. Even dying he did not call me king and struggled with every ounce of energy he had. The skin of his face purpled and his eyes bulged and then he was done. I left his body in the dirt. Scavenger fodder. He deserved worse but there was only so much I could do.

That was the moment I knew my destiny was inevitable, like the sunrise.

I should have buried him. Someone found the corpse and figured I was to blame. Maybe my scent was on him. The others became cautious of me; avoiding me or forming alliances to ward me off or even hunt me.

Using my old skill for stealth I slew two children more despite their watchfulness. One of them I fell upon from a tall tree and stomped them flat with the heels of my feet. The other I caught in a net of vines and stabbed with a twig until they ran out of blood.

After that, the handful who remained made it their mission to vanquish me. They did not understand what they were dealing with.

Deep among the bamboo thickets lurked a cave filled with edible fungus, a place myself and the others sometimes went to scavenge food. There I hid myself in the darkness. I had no idea how long I must wait until one of them happened by, but that was no problem. Freshwater dripped from cracks in the ceiling and I ate the insects that crawled on my skin. My eyes went blind and my joints stiffened. I sat in that hole so long it was as if I was just another stone—or just another log floating in the water, like tarakye was.

A silhouette appeared one day at the cave entrance. They sniffed the air and crept forward until I felt the heat of their body beside me. I yearned to pounce but knew I must wait for the perfect moment. They chewed mushrooms in the gloom and I did nothing. At last, a hand fell upon my knee by accident. Adrenaline thundered into every crevice of my body and I exploded to life. They stood no chance. I bludgeoned their head to paste on the cave wall. Though I craved meat, I feared to eat their flesh lest I absorb their weakness. So I left their body to feed the next crop of mushrooms.

I had more tricks still.

One day I smeared my body with tan clay and plastered bark and leaves to myself. Moving with the speed bamboo grows I removed a nest of wasps from a tree and laid it on the ground. The insects within suspected nothing. I sat out in the open making bird calls to lure my siblings with a tree branch clutched in my hand.

Two of them eventually appeared. They saw me sitting peacefully alongside the nest and must have assumed it was harmless, empty. Both attacked me. I clubbed the wasp nest with the branch and split it open. Deadly buzzing filled the air, a swirling black cloud. Both children fell dead beside me without my ever having to lay a hand on them.

I killed them all in similar ways until only one remained. This one was faster and stronger than me. His existence sent me into fits of fury. None of my tactics worked against him and when he learned I had slain the others he devoted himself to my death, so that I became the one on guard, nervous of shadows and any small noise. I tried everything I could think of without success, until one day I realized it was not enough to simply mimic tarakye: that only tarakye himself could kill my foe.

During the deepest part of night I crept to the lake's rim and sat there until morning when the sun crept above the horizon and the treetops blazed bright like wildfire. At first light I realized a pair of golden eyes watched me from the water's surface, never blinking. I dared not blink either. Intuition warned me that if I did, tarakye would spring from the water and devour me. Flies crawled on my eyeballs, tickling, driving me mad. I did not blink.

"King tarakye," I whispered to the beast, "just wait and you will have your best meal yet."

For three whole days we sat there across from each other unmoving. Tarakye can go weeks or months without feeding. I knew I did not have that much time. Every waking second was agony: numb limbs, clotted blood, stiffened joints, maddening hunger. But I knew if this ploy failed I would only die anyway. So I stayed. I waited.

At sundown my last rival came to the lake. I heard nothing but sensed him behind me. Maybe a whiff of him snuck upwind, or maybe it was a twitch in tarakye's eye.

"Why does it not devour you?" he asked from behind.

"I killed it," I lied.

His toes squelched in the mud behind me.

"How?"

"Poison," I said.

His shadow eclipsed me. There was something long and pointed in his hands. A spear. It hovered above my head, poised to strike.

"The last life you'll take," he said.

I blinked.

Tarakye could just as easily have eaten me. I would not have regretted it. The sight of his obsidian carapace erupting from the water, rows of jagged teeth flashing in the sunlight, was the most beautiful thing I will ever see. His underbelly knocked me to the ground and his mountainous weight almost crushed me and as he retreated back into the water, clutching my hapless rival, his sandpaper hide grazed and bloodied my skin, and then he disappeared with a splash to the sound of a muffled scream. After that, the jungle was quiet again.

*

Zardanis watches me, her face blank, almost like tarakye's reptilian stare except that to me she seems unsure, whereas with tarakye it is always absolutely clear what he wants.

She presses her finger to her ear.

"He's telling the truth," she says. "As he sees it, anyway. I think he really did murder all the others."

I cock my head, trying to tune my ear to the phantom voice.

"All right," she sighs. "Rehabilitation will be costly, though. Can't we just sell him to the slavelords?"

Though this topic seems to be gibberish as well I cannot help but feel some offense is being committed against me.

"We should duel," I suggest, sneering at her muscularity. To me she is bloated, unwieldy. I am smaller but hard and wiry and quick.

Zardanis raises an eyebrow. "You wouldn't stand a chance. Listen carefully, *Tarakye*. Legally I'm not allowed to just terminate you or sell you off. But rehab... well, it's a waste of time, really. I'm going to give you another choice. You can either come back with me—"

I slap my chest with both hands. "Only as king."

"—or, there's a less orthodox option we both might prefer."

That treacherous smile resurfaces. She explains to me what her people are capable of.

*

Sunlight warms me. I tongue the rows of baneful teeth within my jaws. My weight is immense, yet my stout limbs are nothing but saurian muscle. The tail at my flank is a scythe of meat and bone. Hunger smoulders in my belly.

I am elated by my new shape but the emotion is dull and distant, unnecessary for a crocodile.

Movement catches my eye on the shore of the lake—of my kingdom. I act intuitively, sliding into the glassy water. My strength multiplies tenfold now that I am free of gravity's burden. Serpentine motion pushes me through the murk, only my eyes and nostrils exposed to the air.

I am Tarakye, king of the jungle.

Tourists

Jeanne Leppard

Alma swiped at the ethereal finger that prodded her toast.

"Scorched it again I see."

"Go away, Millie. I'm in a hurry."

"What's to get all fussed up about? Plenty of time for good toast and jam."

Millie moved to the other side of the kitchen table, patted down the apron pinned to her dress and plonked herself down on something Alma couldn't see but assumed was a stool. Alma quickly smothered her toast in butter and marmalade and ate it as quickly as possible before Millie decided to prod it again. She was certain that Millie had died of the plague, although she had never asked and Millie had never said. Even so, it made her feel quite unwell to have her food 'touched', if a phantasm could be said to touch anything.

While she chewed, Alma flicked her diary open and frowned at the busy day ahead of her. Her first client would be here for his reading at 9.30am and it was 9 already.

"Busy day is et? A house full of bleedin' ghosts again?" said Millie. She rolled her eyes and made a slow huffing sound of disapproval. "You make sure they don't trample on me vegetables."

"Those infernal vegetables have been dead for more than three hundred years, Millie. No doubt they will spring up anew as they always do once my clients have gone."

She regretted her tone immediately. She felt unusually edgy. She'd spread the cards over the sheets before getting out of bed; a mistake now she came to think about it since the reading was so bad.

Millie stood and turned to look at the kitchen wall behind her, no doubt surveying her vegetables, Alma thought. Millie's little stone cottage spanned Alma's kitchen and just beyond the porch, its width took in her dining room. She couldn't see the cottage most of the time. Only bits of it showed as Millie moved about and gave a translucent life to her beloved home. Alma had moved into the house three years earlier and over that time she had gained a perfect image of the cottage and Millie's sparse furniture. Alma's reading room covered what had been Millie's garden, but she had never seen Millie go there, so she had no idea what vegetables she had grown. She wondered if it was due to her profession, tarot reader and clairvoyant, that Millie never ventured out amongst her beloved plots, but thought not. There was something else she felt that kept Millie from going outside.

Her alarm went off and set her heart racing. Even Millie jumped and looked back at the offending item with a scowl. Gathering up her long skirt, she swept through the kitchen table and the sink that looked out onto Alma's porch and garden – flowers not vegetables.

"I'll be in me livin' room if you want me."

Alma smiled at Millie's back and, grasping her diary, hastened across the hallway into the room in which she worked. She placed the book next to her moneybox on a sideboard against one wall, then opened the curtains and windows to let the sun in and warm the room.

The alarm tinged again in the kitchen and she moved a

little faster. She quickly covered the walls with smoke from her stick of dried sage; the table, both top and bottom, and ran the gathering cloud over the cards and a few crystals that sat upon the mantelpiece.

She waved the stubborn smoke through the windows before closing them and cursed herself for not having prepared the room the night before, especially with a new client coming. Who knew what he'd walk in with? She lit a few tea lights that nestled in little coloured holders and her oil burner into which she drizzled a few drops of mixed oils for harmony and peace; her favourite.

*

"Miss Trill?" asked the tall bent man at her door.

"Mr Cummings. Come in. Call me Alma, please."

She moved aside to let him in. Something prickled against her skin and left a worrying trail of morbidity as he passed. She groaned inwardly; this was going to be a difficult session.

Once seated, Mr Cummings placed the long fingers of his left hand on the table as though for support. He seemed uneasy and leant forward slightly.

As was her way, Alma went straight to the point and asked what she could do for him. Was there anything in particular he wished to explore or would he like a more general reading?

It was about his health he said. "I feel heavy and depressed. My thoughts sometimes seem to belong to another, and my actions also."

As he talked, Alma glimpsed a dark shadow about him. She could see why he felt heavy and depressed. She felt quite miserable just being in the same room. She now realised that she should have burnt something a little more potent, like rosemary or frankincense; harmony and peace wasn't going to cut it with this customer.

She reached for her tarot cards, the Rider pack. The man was still talking.

"It started around the time of that solar flare. You probably remember. About three months ago. Many of my neighbours went into the street to watch. It filled the street with great bursts of light. An incredible sight." He looked down at his hand, which moved with the slight curling of his fingers against the tabletop. "Yes, it was around that time. I went to Charlotte Humble on Merchant Street to see what it was about. I don't know what she did, but I felt fairly normal after. And she gave me such a nice reading. Then about a week ago, the feeling came back. I tried to contact Charlotte, but she didn't return my calls."

He looked up suddenly, aware of what he had said. "Forgive me, Miss Trill—Alma—I didn't mean to suggest you were a fill-in."

"Of course not," she said quickly to ease his concerns. Alma wasn't worried. Charlotte's loss was her gain. Well, perhaps not in this case. She knew Charlotte. A nice lady. She couldn't hear or see the spirits and attracted fewer customers for that reason. But she was a good reader of the signs. She'd call Charlotte later in the day; see if she was okay.

Alma pushed the cards toward him. "Well, let's see what the cards say. Give them a shuffle. Barry isn't it?"

Barry nodded. He reached for the cards. His hands had an overlay of smoky skin. They shook, but he managed not to drop any of the cards and slid the pack toward Alma when he had finished.

Alma stared at the cards for a moment, wondering when her spirit helpers would arrive. They were usually here by now. She glanced up at Barry again. Usually, her clients had a few spirits with them to pass on their messages, but Barry was alone. Their absence made her nervous, but she couldn't wait for them, her client was expecting some form of response to his dilemma.

She placed the cards one by one in her usual spread, then took a deep settling breath and looked down expecting to see them magically reveal Barry's past influences, his present dilemma and the way ahead. But the confusing jumble of nonsense she saw laid out on her table took her breath. She'd never seen a spread like it. Trying not to panic, she called silently to her helpers, but no one came. Barry watched expectantly with a smile that suddenly revealed a younger man behind the wrinkles of his pale face.

Where was his shadow? Barry's whole demeanor had lifted and there was no darkness about him. She glanced about the room: left, right, and looked up at the ceiling. Where was it? Please God, not under the table. Was this what happened when he went to Charlotte for help?

Suddenly, Millie's scream came from the kitchen. Alma bolted upright but didn't leave her seat. Millie was already dead, so she couldn't imagine what further harm could come to her. She forced her attention back to the cards. She thought of getting Barry to shuffle again, but at that moment Millie shot through the door and ran about the room, dodging here and there as though to fend someone off. Then she vanished back into the kitchen, or more likely onto the porch, the far end of her cottage she called her living-room.

The look of terror on Millie's face urged Alma onward. No

time for another shuffle. She made it up, giving him a glowing report, and ushered the man toward the front door as fast as she could. Three separate puffs of wind passed close by her as she was about to close the door. Their passage lifted her fringe and raised the hairs of her body to rigidity. Curious, she put her face through the gap left between door and frame. She thought Barry lurched forward, but he continued through the front gate, so she closed the door quickly and rushed down the hallway.

Millie was nowhere to be seen. She leant over the kitchen sink and peered through the window, so she didn't see him at first. Then her peripheral vision caught sight of his dark shape next to the fridge.

She spun about. She was too frightened to scream or breathe. When her heart started again, it banged for release within her chest and her whole body began to shake.

"What are you doing there?" She squeezed the words through a jaw that refused to move.

The loose dark form waved a hand that was more a puff of loathsome smoke. The movement plucked at her like an icy finger that left her cold and suddenly quite tired.

"You have to leave," she said. Then bit down on the hysteria that was rising within her. Every part of her shrieked a warning. As spirits went, this one was all wrong and she couldn't shake from her mind the image of a black hole within which starlight dies. Now she wanted to cry as well as scream.

"Get rid of 'im," Millie screeched into her left ear.

Alma hadn't felt her approach. She swung about and screamed. Only the look on Millie's face stopped her from shouting.

The alarm from her mobile phone went off again. She

thought she was going to faint but managed to steady herself with a hand on the sink. Her next client was due in fifteen minutes, no time to wrestle with this apparition or Millie's fears. Nor her own, she realised.

She pulled herself upright and waved her finger at the black figure.

"You stay there, I'll sort you out when I've seen this client." She swiveled about to find herself staring into Millie's face only inches away. "And you go and sit in your living room. Do some knitting or something."

Alma rushed into her reading room and shakily tipped a quantity of frankincense crystals onto a charcoal block in a metal burner, then set light to them. The smell was overwhelming, but it made her feel better. Frankincense was said to have exorcistic qualities and should keep the beast from hell at bay. It may even filter into the kitchen and send him away, but she doubted that it was going to be that easy.

*

The young man who stepped through the front door laughed and chattered as Alma made surreptitious attempts to rush him along. The chattering stopped when they entered the fume-filled reading room. The man's voice stopped in his throat and he coughed politely into his hand. Alma's eyes began to water. She would have asked her client to take a seat if she could have spoken. Opening the window helped. She wondered what had possessed her to put so many crystals into the burner. She put the offending item on the sill and closed the window when the air was breathable again.

As before, her helpers were absent as were the spirits of

the dead that normally accompanied her clients, and she began to wonder if it was due to the abomination sitting next to her fridge. She put thoughts of her unwelcome guest aside and concentrated on the cards that she had laid down in a spread upon the table. She didn't remember doing it, nor her client shuffling them. *Mindfulness*, she said to herself. *Be present.*

A little voice in her head answered: *good luck with that.* She ignored it.

Alma stared at the cards and realized that she had become too reliant on all the spirit helpers. The spread was a little worrying, but not so hard—unlike Barry's.

The young man chattered happily enough as he followed Alma to the door. She smiled and nodded, but most of her attention was taken by the Problem in her kitchen. She thought she could hear Millie jabbering to someone.

Her client had nearly reached the gate when the breezes shot past again. The man tripped and briefly studied the path to see what had made him stumble.

Alma closed the door and quietly counted the number of individual breezes that had passed: four.

Back in the kitchen, the Problem was still there guarding her fridge. She gulped down a glass of water at the sink and glared at Millie who appeared startled. *Feeling guilty at befriending the enemy,* Alma thought.

Her alarm went off again and her hand spasmed with a desire to throw it on the floor and pound it with the meat tenderiser. She squeezed out a smile at Millie, the best she could manage in the circumstances, and rushed up the hall to the front door—her midday client was early.

*

The same scenario played out with her third client: a great gust of wind followed them out the front door. She had sped through their reading and eased them out early, charging them half the normal fee.

Lunchtime came at last. She filled a burner with frankincense crystals, fired them up and took the smoking mess into the kitchen.

"Go home," she shouted at Millie and jiggled the burner about as incentive before dumping it loudly on the table.

Millie fled to the other end of her room; the Problem waved a dark wispy hand about again, sending a chill through her body and made a huffing sound that could have been a cough if he'd had lungs and wasn't so translucent.

She needed air. She walked out onto the front step and took a sharp left to avoid the pathway. Scooted over the low fence to the car and rummaged about in the glove box for the packet of cigarettes she kept there for moments of weakness, or emergencies such as this, and sat in the car doorway with her feet on the pavement. Her left hand pattered on her forehead.

What was she going to do? She wasn't very good at this kind of thing: sending malevolent entities to the light, or wherever they wanted to go. And then there was the wind! What was it? Or more precise, what were they? Nothing good, she was certain of that at least.

She could ring around, see if someone would come and help, but she'd left her phone in the house. She should probably cancel all appointments until she had gotten rid of the Problem and worked out what the breezes were. But! She needed the money. She'd wait and see if it would resolve itself, and in the meantime, call Charlotte and see how she had dealt with it.

"Are you thinking of joining us?" came a clear voice from

the back seat.

Alma swivelled about and glared at the partially-formed features of Tina, a middle-aged woman with long hair resting on the faux leopard skin seat covers. She'd lived up the street and died a few years earlier and now dropped by occasionally for a chat. "You won't be able to get rid of it, you know."

No, she didn't know. *Stay calm and be nice.* "Why not?"

"Because he's not dead, darling." Gary, also from down the street, always had that honk-honk intonation about his voice. There was something a little slimy about Gary and she preferred he didn't appear, although he could be very useful on occasion.

Alma stared at him. "Of course, he's dead."

Tina shifted to the side a little, away from Gary who sat too close. They smiled in unison and shook their heads slowly as though joined at the jaw. Her confidence in the condition of the Problem wavered a little.

"Ooer!" said Gary. He ducked his head as though to avoid something. "Traffic's really bad on this side. Better go."

"What do you mean, 'traffic's bad'?"

But her attention had already shifted to a middle-aged man with grey hair about to push through her gate.

"Shit. Is it two already?" Alma looked at her watch. Where had the time gone? She hadn't had lunch, or prepared the room, and now she smelt of cigarettes. She heaved herself up with the intention of walking toward him, when a crowd of spirits began to gather on her pathway as though the denseness of their numbers would prevent his progress. They moved about him in agitated waves, family members by the likeness of their features.

She was fairly sure he couldn't see them, but their presence must have pressed on some inner sense and he turned about and walked quickly back down the street.

Alma was both relieved and cross and she took a moment to pat down her disappointment and money fears before proceeding to the front gate. She still had two more clients, she reasoned, and it had been an unusually busy day.

Sirens and lights streaked past along the High Street at the end of her street. She lingered, watching. There must have been a terrible accident somewhere. It suddenly occurred to her that they had been going past all day.

The pub across the road had begun to fill up. The steady trickle of people who walked past were probably heading for the pub up on the next corner. Friday afternoon was always a busy time. Flexible work hours meant an early start to the joys of the weekend for many.

She turned down the path toward her front door. Somehow, she knew the Problem was still there. She could feel it. She pushed down her panic with a deep breath. What if she couldn't get rid of it? She was freaked out enough already, and it was still daylight. What if it was still there tonight when it was dark? She couldn't possibly sleep knowing that thing lurked in her kitchen and might decide, at any moment, to explore the rest of her house, especially if it wasn't dead. She'd ring Charlotte as soon as she had retrieved her phone. She could always sleep at a friend's for a night or two.

For a moment she thought she'd locked herself out, but the door gave at a push and swung back against the wall with a bang.

The wind that tunnelled down the hallway lifted her off her feet and deposited her against the fence that separated her front garden from the next-door neighbour. It gave way, more from the force of her landing than her weight. Her head thudded on the grass, leaving her a little dizzy as well as winded.

She lay still; too frightened to move. Her heart clanged like church bells on a Sunday morning. She could feel the wind passing over her legs; tactile. It reminded her of the fast-moving wind that underground trains pushed through their small tunnels; invisible but with a force that could blow you over. A sound like excited, high-pitched chatter emanated from the wind and vibrated around her.

When the chattering wind tunnel had passed, she didn't feel capable of rising, and when the dark wispy shadow crept over her, she knew it was too late. The strength in her muscles ran like water into the grass, and tears of terror and defeat ran either side of her head and into her hair. The Problem leant over her, closer and closer. It made noises she couldn't understand. It smelt, but with a smell that her senses couldn't comprehend, and the texture of its substance defied any understanding.

*

Alma had no idea just how long she had lain there amongst the ruin of her fence. The sounds of revelry coming from the pub was now dissipating with the progress of evening. With a groan, she finally pulled herself up and crept through the door and leant on the wall for support as she made her way towards the kitchen.

She knew it wasn't there but looked anyway. Millie sat on an old wooden chair, warming herself in front of the fridge, where flames danced like a hologram on the fridge door.

Exhausted, Alma pulled out a chair and sagged over the table.

"Been goin' on for days; people missin' en' dyin'," Millie said quite suddenly. Her lack of concern appalled Alma. "Watched it on next door's telly."

"You went next door!"

"It's where me privy is."

"Privy! Millie, please don't tell me you think you still need to use the privy." Alma found herself laughing, a little out of control.

Millie turned from her hand warming and smiled. "They used to call 'em faery 'oles. Not privies, the 'oles where people disappeared. All over the country they were. In foreign parts too, I 'eard. Lots of 'em in our village. Different this time though. Fings coming out, not people goin' in. Come up one 'ole en' go back in anuver."

A faery hole—next to her fridge; Millie's old hearth! Millie hadn't died of the plague. It had all been to do with this 'faery hole' as she called it; places where people were said to disappear without trace. Things had been through there before. She knew Millie was right, the alien wind of beings came through the portals, danced and sang with their hosts, then left via a different portal.

How did she know this? The answer was elusive. It slipped away as forgotten things sometimes do just when you're on the brink of remembering the answer. She knew also, in the same strange way, that all the hosts were dead; sucked dry of their vital energy.

She suddenly remembered what Barry had said: "My thoughts sometimes seem to belong to another, and my actions also". She looked down at her arm, her panic rising like the bile in her throat, but she saw nothing.

Alma sat on a garden chair on the porch with her bare feet jutting out beyond the shade to warm up in the glorious spring sun. Beside her, Millie relaxed in her old worn armchair knitting the same pair of socks she'd been knitting for hundreds of years. Alma sighed happily and sipped on her tea. She'd boiled the water over a pit fire Millie had taught her to make. She had been without electricity for over a week with no hope of it ever returning. The chickens she had rescued from the house down the road scratched and clucked about her garden, adding a sense of peace to the moment.

The sky was a clear blue, the air felt fresh and clean and floral perfumes drifted on gentle breezes. The sound of traffic had stopped a week ago and the sound of birdsong rang loudly in the air.

A dark shadow rippled over Alma's bare arm, accompanied by visions of destructive revellers rampaging through humanity. She wondered when he would return to wherever he had come from and seek out another holiday destination. Then she and Millie would be alone—for eternity, perhaps! Or until the sun swallowed them up.

Her body shivered with another dark ripple.

Millie dropped her knitting.

"Tourists," said Alma.

The End of the World

Dan Robb

Dust-stained and aching, I came to the end of the world.

I trembled, fell to my knees on the rock peninsula and gazed into the star-littered black. Behind me to the left and right, oceans flowed over the edge to swirl and freeze and drift into space. The still air tasted bitter; silence rang in my ears. No creature ventured there.

I had made it. My journey, my life's work, was done. Voices from the past hounded me — "ruthless", "obsessed", "fool" — but I had proven them wrong. Barely more than a babe when I set out, now old and tired, I had finally come to the end of the world.

Crawling forward over coarse stone, I thought of those I had left behind. Comrades, friends, enemies; those distracted by women, those hobbled by children, those waylaid by games or music or books; those who had not made it. I had made it. My fist closed around a sharp stone, smoother and darker than the rest; left there, it seemed, just for me. And gratefully I would use it. I would carve my name into the stone at the very peak of the rock so that the universe would know that I alone had made it. And then I would take my final step.

But upon reaching the peak, beneath which there was only cold and dark, I halted. Dismayed. Where I would place my name there were names already. A multitude of names. As many as the stars beyond. I knelt there, head bowed, breath ragged; until with a dazed hand I could scrawl my initials in a small space between others. Then I rose to complete my journey.

I thought again of the people I had left behind. I wondered whether they still thought of me. I wondered whether they would envy me. "No." I realised as I stood alone at the end of my life, I didn't think that they would.

My toes hung over the end of the rock, ice crystals forming around them. I felt the pull of the distant stars and wondered what lay beyond. *Could I stop? Could I turn back?*

I had reached the end of the world. Was that not the point of it all?

"Is it too late to turn back?"

The response, like an echo from the stars. *Turn back. Turn back.*

The Last Bag of Beans

G. N. Warren

It came to pass that the world ran out of coffee.

Some blamed the coffee shop glut; others blamed the millennials for their obsession with coffee shops. Many blamed various acts of the Inconveniently Multiplicitous One and Only True God.

For a brief time, it was suggested climate change was the culprit, but this was dismissed immediately by the coal and oil barons. As this view was only challenged by a few greenies, school kids, scientists and politicians not on the payroll, it was quickly accepted that the fires, floods, droughts, diseases and mass extinctions were perfectly natural.

Whatever the cause, the world was down to one single bag of medium roast Arabica discovered in the final effects of a thoroughly unremarkable ex-barista named Dave.

As a condition of his will, Dave required that the bag of beans be gifted to one lucky citizen of the world. This citizen was to be selected from a list of all emails that had ever been hacked by the Chinese.

It is due to this strange series of events (and the lax security practices of Gardener's Monthly to which he'd subscribed for 25 years) that Mr. Barry Cheshire of South Westin, New South Wales, found himself the centre of global attention.

It was a fine Wednesday morning when Barry walked out into his front yard to collect the junk mail. He was surprised and confused to be greeted by a view not of the dusty and deserted main street of South Westin, but of the local police sergeant holding a small cardboard box, and behind him a noisy line of people stretching far off into the distance.

"What's going on here, Sarge?" Barry asked.

The police sergeant quickly told the story of what was in the box.

"A bag of coffee beans, how wonderful," Barry said. "So, who are all these people?"

"They are all citizens of the world, coming to petition you to hand over that bag of coffee beans."

"Oh, I don't know about that," Barry said. "These beans will—"

A sudden commotion in the line drowned out Barry's words as a strange orange man, bobbing on a golden throne hovering above the crowd, pushed and yelled his way to the front. As the strange orange man got closer, Barry could see the throne was sitting on a litter borne by a dozen or more men, some dressed in soldiers' uniforms, others in grey banker's suits. In between bursts of abuse, the orange man worked frantically on a phone with his small, childlike hands.

"I am King Donald of the Wholly Subjugated States of America," the man said as he got to the front of the now angry crowd. "And I have a deal for you."

King Donald thrust a book into Barry's hands.

"What is this?" Barry said.

"It's my new book: *How to Buy Friends and Fool People.*

It's going to be a classic. I will swap you for the coffee beans."

Barry looked askance at the book. "Never been much for reading myself, more of a headlines and sports pages kind of guy, but thank you for the offer." Barry handed the book back to King Donald, who went a slightly redder shade of orange before ordering his litter bearers to turn around, tapping his phone with renewed ferocity.

The next group in the line were all old men dressed in rich robes, jewelled and embroidered in gold. They all wore a range of hats, from small, unassuming caps, to grand pointy affairs with more jewels and more gold. Each man was trying his best to look down his nose at the others, which was quite comical as some were much shorter than the others.

One of the men stepped forward, their leader Barry assumed by virtue of him having the tallest, pointiest hat. "I represent the Multitudinous Representatives of the Inconveniently Multiplicitous One and Only True God," the man said. "We will forgive your sins and offer you a guaranteed place in heaven in return for your bag of coffee beans."

"No thanks," Barry said.

The man looked confused, "But you will go to hell and burn in fire for all eternity if you refuse our offer. Heaven is your only salvation."

"There'll be virgins." A voice piped up from behind the man.

"There has only ever been one woman for me," Barry said. "My May was the kindest, most wonderful person in the world. She never harmed a fly. I have also been the best man I can be. If there is something beyond this world and you're saying that we can't go there without joining you lot with your bowing and your praying and your killing each other, then so be it. The answer is still no."

As the old men moved away, it revealed most of the noise in the crowd was coming from the group of well-dressed men next in line, all shouting at each other in different languages. After a moment or six, a dapper gent at the front noticed Barry standing there and stepped forward.

"My apologies, Mr. Cheshire," the dapper gent said with a heavy French accent. "We are the Heads of the Disunited Rabble Formally Known as the European Union. We came here to make you a great offer for your bag of coffee beans, but none of us could agree on what that offer should be, so I'll think we'll just leave."

As the well-dressed men moved off, next in line was the strangest sight Barry had ever seen. Atop a low, four-wheeled platform, an extremely lifelike statue of an ancient-looking man sat astride what appeared to be a gilded megaphone.

"Good morning, Mr. Cheshire," the statue said, its voice booming from the megaphone and frightening the daylights out of Barry.

A younger and much more alive-looking man stepped from behind the statue, "Sorry, Mr. Cheshire, I didn't mean to startle you there. I am Lachlan, Son and Official Mouth Puppet of the Late Mr. Murdoch, Master of All Truth, Stuffed and Mounted for Eternity."

"Hello, Lachlan," Barry said. "Did you know your late father appears to be talking out his bottom?"

"Yes, he was good at that, but I digress—if you give me your bag of beans, I can make anything you desire to be true become truth. Don't like your neighbour? No worries, we can make him a terrorist and have him put away. Don't want a politician to win? We can make sure everyone believes they're in league with Satan or born in another country. Heck, we can even make you a king, like King Donald."

Barry was aghast. "That just sounds dishonest to me. And I don't want to be like King Donald, I just want to live in peace here in my own home."

Lachlan leaned forward and jabbed a pointy finger at Barry's chest. "You'll regret this, Mr. Cheshire. The headlines never lie, and tomorrow your name is mud. And if you try to say any different, we'll just call it fake news, and you'll be even worse off."

Barry grabbed Lachlan's finger and pushed him away. "Sergeant, can you escort this young man and his stuffed father away, please."

As the police sergeant led them away, Barry had a strong urge to go wash his hands but was distracted by the strange pair next in line.

Both men were well into middle age but dressed in t-shirts and jeans and sneakers like they'd just left school. They introduced themselves as Messrs Zuckerberg and Dorsey, Global Arbiters of Friendship and Self-Worth.

"I can get you a million followers," said one.

"I can have two million people hanging off your every tweet," said the other.

"What's a tweet?" said Barry.

"You'll have millions of friends!" The two shirted and sneakered men cried, ignoring Barry's question.

"What would I do with a million friends?" Barry said. "This is only a small town, where would I fit them all?"

"Oh, you don't ever meet them," the men said. "All your friends will be online."

"You mean on the computer?"

"Yes, and on your smartphone," the men said.

"I have a phone, but I don't think it's very smart—it has buttons and hangs on the wall," Barry said.

"We'll give you a smartphone. Then you can take your friends everywhere."

"That sounds really silly to me. Friends are people you share a beer with, a weekly game of cards, and sometimes even your deepest hopes and fears. You can't carry friends in a pocket." Barry shrugged an apology. "I don't think I'd like even one of these online friends you talk about, let alone a million of them."

The next group in the line were more finely dressed men, this time standing around a group of expensive sports cars. A couple of the men had women with them that Barry would have guessed to be their granddaughters if it wasn't for the very un-granddaughterly way they were hanging off the men. The women wore more gold than all of the old men in hats combined.

"We are the League of Distinguished Billionaires," the most finely dressed of them all said. "We will give you a billion dollars and membership to our club in exchange for your bag of beans."

"What would I do will a billion dollars?" Barry asked.

"Why, you could own all this and more," the man waved in the general direction of the sports cars and the women.

"For starters, one of those things wouldn't last a week before the roads out here tore out the suspension," Barry said, being very careful to point at the cars and not the women. "And I am sure I would not be comfortable with a whole lot of money I didn't earn."

"Aah, a traditional man, I see," said another of the men,

stepping forward to greet Barry. "Very good, we can also teach you about this fantastic caper called trickle-down economics, where you do a little work and get to receive great floods of money while everyone else gets a trickle."

"No. Thank. You," Barry folded his arms and shook his head in the most definitive manner he could muster.

On and on it went, for most of the day, but not one of the people in the line could offer Barry something that would convince him to part with his bag of beans. Finally, only the police sergeant, Barry and an elderly man with a computer tablet and a satchel stood at Barry's gate.

"And what do you want to offer me for my beans?" Barry asked the elderly man, his shoulders slumped with weariness.

"Oh, I'm not here for your beans, I am an intern from the Daily Waffle News Channel."

"You look a bit old for an intern," Barry observed.

"Oh, they only call us interns so they don't have to pay us," the man said. "I've worked on the news desk for 37 years."

"So why are you here?"

"I'm here for the story—I want to know why none of these people could convince you to part with those beans?"

Barry perked up and smiled. "I was wondering if anyone was ever going to ask. Come inside, and I will show you."

Barry led the reporter into his tired but tidy kitchen and fished an ancient coffee grinder and stovetop percolator from a cupboard. "Please, take a seat," Barry pointed to a small, well-worn dining table with two chairs, but set for one.

As Barry carefully ground a cup full of beans and set the percolator to brew, the kitchen filled with a delicious aroma that reminded the reporter of man buns and smashed avocado and stupid American sitcoms about friends who hated each other.

When the percolator gave a final burp and a hiss, Barry lifted it carefully off the stove, sniffed the coffee once, and said, "Would you like a cup?"

"Oh, my, yes!" the reporter said, his eyes now watering to match his mouth at such an honour.

Barry pulled down a plain, impeccably white coffee cup and matching saucer from another cupboard and carefully poured the dark liquid into the cup. "Milk and sugar?" he asked.

"Just black is fine."

Barry placed the coffee on the table. The reporter, whose whole body was now threatening to go to water just at the heady smell of the coffee, reached out a tremulous hand, lifted the cup and took a sip.

Suddenly, a billion tired and worn neurons fired at once and the reporter's brain filled with 1000 plots, a hundred novels, and at least one cure for all that was ill in the world. As his mental planets and stars and galaxies and universes aligned in a crescendo of ecstasy, there weren't enough superlatives in all of the languages of the world to express how he felt. Instead, he stuck with time-honoured tradition and let out a deep, satisfied *aaaaahhh*.

When the reporter had nearly finished the brew, Barry topped the cup up with the remaining coffee.

"You not having a cup?" the reporter asked.

"Oh, I don't really like coffee," Barry said.

"But…but, I don't understand."

Barry picked the now empty percolator up and stepped to the back door. "Come," he said. "Bring your coffee."

Barry led the reporter out into a garden full of life and dazzling variety, the likes of which the reporter had only ever seen in books and documentaries. A narrow path of pavers, worn and sunken in the middle from decades of use wove between rows of garden beds and myriad pots of all sizes. Everywhere you turned, there was a riot of colour. Sweet fragrances and the gentle hum of bees and insects hung in the air.

"My May passed two years ago this week," Barry explained as he led the reporter through the garden. "It was a slow process for her, and this garden was her sanctuary. In the end, when it got too much for her, she'd sit in her chair out here, and we'd just talk for hours about our lives and what we had together."

Barry's eyes grew misty, but the slight smile did not leave his face. "When we made that final trip to the hospital, May had to leave this house and her garden and all that we had together behind, but she took those memories with her."

Barry's eyes grew hard again as he thrust his chin towards the front of the house. "What those silly, shallow people out front today don't realise is that none of that stuff matters. You can have all the money and cars and boats and partners and stuff in the world, but you can't take it with you. In the end, all any of us can take with us in those last moments are the memories of the life we lived."

Barry led the reporter to a row of low shrubs packed with waxy, dark green leaves and awash with soft, velvety white flowers. A subtle aroma that reminded the reporter of grandmothers and tea and homemade biscuits wafted up from the bushes.

"May's gardenias," Barry said. "They were her favourite. My fondest memories of May all revolve around them. I remember she was always saying the same thing, 'Barry, gardenias are not as hard to keep alive as people think. You just have to remember rule number one…'"

Barry upended the percolator, dumping the spent contents on the bushes. "'Gardenias love coffee grinds.'"

Broadmeadows

Mary Harrington

It was my tenth summer working at Broadmeadows station. My uncle had got me the job as he'd worked for the railway for the last forty years. In the big war, it was his job to direct all the grain and produce from the country to rendezvous with ships taking it the rest of the way around the world.

After the third pandemic, jobs are scarce. Four billion lost souls meant crucial jobs were gone, including food production. Governments couldn't train people fast enough. The Pig flu had targeted mainly young people, 20-40. This meant all the trades were decimated. You couldn't get a plumber or an electrician or someone to build your house. All civil engineering and infrastructure works had stopped almost overnight. Hell, the people we had fixing our trains and tracks would be pensioned off by now.

Now everyone worked long hours in every area. Injury rates were high, as well as euphemisms such as 'lack of trackside compliance'. Transport was an essential service and now deemed National Security, so we were worked harder than most and we often worked sick or injured.

My family had been relatively unscathed. We lived out of town, on a sprawling, remote property that ran cattle and sheep. With our twins, that made four generations in three homesteads.

Broadmeadows was far from everywhere. If you were

going somewhere it would be three seconds of light, in the wide expanse of pure darkness that blasted past you, until the clickety-clack dragged you back to your dreams of wide flat desolate plains.

Broadmeadows was the central point making all the other Nowheres accessible. The station was also a large shunting yard, dark and full of sudden clanging noises as trains were rerouted to all points of the compass. Rail workers plying their silent, unseen toil in high-vis vests made useless in the gloom, far from civilization and even daylight—all in the name of shift work, shifting both hours and trains.

Something was up. The schedules and descriptions of freight coming through were usually wordy to the extent you would tune out. T44's only description was NTK NATSEC. Need to know: a new luxury most couldn't afford. This meant very tight deadlines, often military, pushing the trains around it out of schedule while introducing randomness to a routine, rigid network. Believe me, surprises were the last thing you wanted when dealing with 18,000 tons of metal moving at speed towards you. This one had two engines in front so possibly even heavier, or faster.

T44 was an 'up' train heading east and had priority over all west or down or odd-numbered trains. We had ten minutes to safely put four down trains on our four passing sidings. The first would be here in 2 minutes 36 seconds. The radio crackled again. "T33 to Broadmeadows, I'm reading a signal failure at marker 357. Is it showing on your control panel?"

Tom, Alex's uncle, was still the controlling officer; he picked up the radio. "Nothing showing here. I'll go out on the bike and have a look.

"I'll toss you for it, if you like", said Alex, nodding towards the well-used dart board in the middle of the room. "I'll sweeten the pot and make it double or nothing." Alex was better on the bikes and tried to protect his uncle who was getting on, by trying to take these jobs. "You first" he teased.

Tom threw a beautifully executed and perfectly aimed dart that hit the bullseye slightly too hard and immediately bounced out. "Looks like I'll be going up the hill" Tom drawled.

Signals failed because of cable theft, a fuse blowing, or the points not locking into place. He tapped his trusty self-made mini tool kit on his belt for luck; the same as the one he made for Alex. The first train was piloted into the first siding by Gary, the shunting operator. *No dramas* thought Alex.

The second train was longer than expected—which shouldn't happen, but did, too often. It was guided smoothly into the third spot which was slightly larger than the rest.

All of a sudden, people started spilling out both sides onto the tracks. They were work refugees, unskilled people looking for low-level work, called job gypsies.

Alex bolted from the control room, grabbed Gary and said, "We need to get them into the paddock now!" This was the most dangerous type of work environment and they were short staffed.

All the while, Alex was looking over his shoulder wondering when the next train was coming. The howl of the warning whistle rang out. They screamed "RUN" at the top of their lungs. The points were already set. The train was here.

Gary grabbed a woman and child, the last stragglers, pushing them to safety. Gary wasn't so lucky, though, as the train clipped his ankle, sending him flying. Luckily for him, it wasn't caught under the wheels, as there was no medical treatment for hundreds of kilometres. The gypsies were making their own way out of town and Alex quickly took Gary back to the control room.

"Looks like bad bruising" Alex said, "so you'll have to stay here."

The warning alarm sounded for the priority train coming. Alex grabbed the radio and ran to the points to reset them. He used all his strength to reset them quickly.

The radio screamed. "This is T44 we are making an unscheduled stop!"

"Roger," Alex puffed.

"Tom to control, points fixed and train coming through now." T33 made it to the siding with seconds to spare. Alex raced to the platform as T44 screeched in. A lone NAT SEC officer with sweat pouring off him stepped off T44.

"I need your help, are you good on the tools? A nuclear device is activated, and we have two hours to deactivate it while getting it to nowhere, are you in?"

The Ice Against the Heart

Christopher Williams

This is what I know:

My name is Teddy Twissel.
My real name is Theodore.
I am ten years old.
I've lost my mum. She's disappeared.
My best friend Gumbo lives in my pocket.
My other friends live on the internet.
The internet is not working.
My new friend Isabel lives with me now. She is nine.
I am not retarded.

THEN

Dad yelled a swear word and the door banged shut. That loud noise made me freeze up inside. Like ice. I remembered mum crying and I wanted to pat her arm, her face, anything that would make it better. I couldn't. I was frozen.

Now mum is gone. She's disappeared.

My name is Theodore but everyone calls me Teddy. I woke up one morning almost a year ago and my mum was not here. This is my story. I'm writing it down so I won't forget anything 'cause words might make more sense than the pictures I generally use to remember things. Inside my head, that is. Sorry if this story is a bit mixed up but I'm writing it down as it comes out of my head, sort of all jumbled up kind of.

I lived with my mum in our house called *GREENHE VEN*. Someone must have stolen the *'A'* before we moved here. And Tilly. That's our ginger cat. Our house has a green door which banged a lot when dad was living here. It has a green roof, seventeen windows and 522 bricks on one wall and 2,150 bricks on another. I know 'cause I counted them. When I was six.

Izzy lives with me now. She is nine. I talk to my other best friend Gumbo every day. He sleeps under my pillow. He is green and I can bend him a little if I'm feeling angry. He says that's OK cause it doesn't hurt. Not like my dad hurt. He left when I was five.

We live in a town called Jackaranda in a street behind the shops. We have a neighbour called Mr Engelman who loves his roses. He lets me call him Mr E. He is my friend too. I used to go to Jackaranda Public School but I think it's closed now. I was in year 4. I miss my teacher, Miss Jackson. She used to let me sit up next to her and be her special helper, handing out the pens and paper, making sure nobody was shouting. She let me wear my special headphones so quiet music played when it got noisy. Which it did a lot. I don't like Timmy Jones. He would try and trip me over and take away my truck. He had freckles and smelt like the toilet at the park, the one that no one ever flushes.

Mr Engelman calls me *Theo my boy*. He is old and mum said he was *senile*. I looked up that word on my computer, when it was working, and it means *showing the weakness of old age, especially a loss of mental faculties* but that can't be what Mr E has because he's not weak and never forgets my name. I told him he can call me Teddy but the next day he just said: *Hello, Theo my boy.* Sometimes he calls me *young man.* I guess he might think I'm older than ten but I don't mind if he thinks that.

Mr E had a carer who helped him shower and brought his meals. She was a nice lady who used to smile and wave at me sometimes. Her name was Mrs De Paul. She drove a man's car because it had *Vincent* written on the side.

Me and Izzy have to do all that now.

My mum's name is Carol. She disappeared last year with everyone else. Except Mr E. and Alice and Isabel. Maybe it was like in the *Avengers* when Thanos clicked his fingers and lots of people turned into dust. But I don't think that's what happened 'cause I didn't see any alien spaceships in the sky.

My dad used to yell at me and call me mean names, so Mum asked him to leave. Once when I was littler, I heard them shouting at each other. *Leave, just leave! She yelled.* He was saying the naughty *R* word which I think was *retarded.* She said: *That's not true. He's barely on the spectrum!* I think that's why dad left. I looked up the *R* word and I know that's not me 'cause I've never been *held back.*

I knew when I was in trouble because mum called me *Theodore*, not Theo or Teddy. I love my mum 'cause she looked after me and Gumbo and made sure Gumbo didn't get wet. One time he got wet and felt all slimy and I know I wouldn't like to feel like that. Mum loved Gumbo too because she put him under my pillow every night when I went to sleep.

The day that mum disappeared, Mr E was in his garden, cutting his roses like nothing was any different. He lives with Alice now. We found Alice at the Police Station looking for her wallet. There were no policemen there. Or policewomen. They must have left in a hurry because they left their guns there. Her wallet was not there either.

Today is Sunday. I know this because mum has a calendar in the kitchen and I cross the days off every day. So on Sundays I sleep in. Mum used to do that. She slept in the room next to me and we have special pillows. Now Isabel, who I call Izzy, sleeps there. I have Batman on my pillows and she has Wonder Woman on hers. This is because my nanna Stella used to say all the time: *Carol, you are a wonderful woman.* I love my nanna Stella. She always gave me a present when she came to visit. Last time she gave me a Batman belt which is a bit small but I wear it anyway. Nannas can't always know your size, can they?

The internet worked for a few days then stopped. The microwave wasn't working either. The power must have turned off. Or maybe my mum didn't pay her electricity bill 'cause she was talking about the *bloody power company* the day before she disappeared. I think that's a swear word. Mum never swore except when the car wouldn't start she yelled: *start, you worthless piece of shit!* Sometimes that worked. But not often. She then called a mechanic who is a man who knows how to start cars without swearing.

I fixed the power. Dad left some tools in the back shed. They were all lined up neatly in order in the box. That made my brain feel nice and calm. He left a book about fixing things and a book about wires and electricity. We had solar panels on our roof 'cause mum said we got a *big discount.* I cut the cable in our meter box thingy (the cable that the power company was using to steal our solar power) using Mr E's secateurs. I wore mum's rubber gloves so I wouldn't die. It worked.

I can hear Tilly meowing outside. Mum said I could have a puppy for my next birthday. And another truck. I've got green, red, blue racing trucks and a black monster truck. Green is my favourite colour. But I don't think puppies come in green.

There are a few stray dogs that come around and we feed them leftovers, if we have any. Some are scary and growl. We don't ever feed those. We don't have any meat 'cause it got too smelly at the IGA store.

I thought at first that mum had gone for a keep-in-shape walk to find Mr Right she'd been talking about. I hope she doesn't find somebody who wants to yell at me. I still miss dad, but I don't want to see him in case he yells at me. I don't like loud noises. They make me kind of freeze up inside in a bad kind of way, not in a nice ice creamy-kind of way. Maybe she got lost or turned left or something because she used to always say to me: *Teddy, you never know what's around the corner.* I knew though. It was the IGA store!

I went to see if Mr E knew where my mum was. I didn't tell him that she thought he was *senile* because that word doesn't sound nice. He was over the fence trimming his roses with his secateurs. He said he loves roses because they remind him of Miriam. I think that was his wife. Or maybe his mum. He won't tell me, he just says *my precious Miriam* like she's something he lost or doesn't want to break. My mum used to say dad broke her heart when he'd yell at me. I used to wonder how she fixed it up again 'cause Mr E said Miriam died of a broken heart.

I said then:

"Hi, Mr Engelman. Have you seen my mum 'cause I've lost her?"

"Hello, Theo my boy. Lost your mum? Matter of fact, I

don't remember seeing Miriam lately, have you seen her?"

"Remember, she died a long time ago? Sorry Mr E."

"Of course. That's OK, Theo my boy. I'm sure we'll find your mum. Let's take a walk downtown to the IGA. I'm sure we'll find her there. Mothers have to shop a lot, don't they?"

And that's how it all started. Our search for my mum.

LATER

We turned left from Mr E's gate down King street past empty cars, some with motors still running, others with doors wide open as if their drivers forgot something. We walked past shopping bags left stranded while dogs ripped open cartons of meat. Cats lapped at melting ice cream, the Neapolitan colours had mixed together in a muddy puddle. We walked past the bakery with the nice smell. There were cup-cakes, donuts and slices all lined up in neat rows waiting. Then we walked past a place mum called the pub. It had a funny smell. Mum said that's where men go when they want to forget stuff. I stopped and held Mr E's hand which was warm and soft like a baby's, not cold and hard like I imagined.

We walked wide eyed in silence as the wind blew empty plastic bags down the street that got stuck on spiky fence pickets and tree branches. The emptiness was both scary and nice at the same time. Before, life was full of harsh noises and blank faces. It was the faces that scared me the most, not knowing what was behind them. Sometimes they said kind words but the faces were saying the opposite. It's easier now they've all gone. Mr E's face is blank mostly until he sees me then it lights up. That's how I know he is my friend.

I've never seen anything like this, not even on Netflix. I watched it when I thought mum wasn't watching. I don't like being sneaky but Mum doesn't let me watch anything with violence or Zombies. I loved *Ozark* the best, especially the boy Mike Fleming, not his real name, who could hide money in offshore accounts. They must be like islands somewhere where you can hide things like the pirates used to. One day I'll do that with my computer. When the internet is back on. But I think mum knew. She knows everything. Or she used to. Like how to cook my pasta sauce just right, not too hot, not too runny, how to iron my clothes so that the creases always go in the right places, how hot to run my bath. But not always how to start her car. I have to do all that now.

Sometimes Izzy helps me but I have to tell her lots. I think she might be on the spectrum too, just in a different part.

(Sorry, I got a little distracted. Back to the story.)

We came to a 7-Eleven store.

"You feeling hungry, Mr E?"

"No, Theo my boy, I'm thirsty. Get us a lemonade please. Here's five dollars."

I went to the drink fridge with the five dollars and got two cans of lemonade, one for me. There was no one to pay, so I left the money next to the cash register and thought of writing a note but didn't see any pens. So I put the money in the donations jar for lost dogs. Mum used to say: *If you steal, karma will get you.* I think he's like a policeman for stealers.

We walked down the street towards the IGA. My mum used to say: *Let's go to I Got Apples* when we had to go shopping. That's how I knew where we were going. When the car started. She never left me alone. Once she told me of a mum who left her little boy at home alone and when she got home the house was on fire 'cause the little boy put something bad in the microwave. I'm not sure if that's a real story or a made up one, just to scare me into not touching dangerous things like snakes and spiders and guns. I was never allowed to use the microwave. Mum was going to teach me soon.

The street outside the IGA was empty. It looked like a spooky Hollywood documentary I saw once. I waited at the intersection to cross the road for the light to go green but there were no lights. So I just waited.

"C'mon, Theo my boy, I'm hungry."

Outside there were two shopping trolleys with their front wheels in the gutter. I took a trolley and pushed it inside.

"Follow me Mr E."

"Miriam brings me here. Do you think she might be here?"

"Don't think so, Mr E. Looks like there's nobody here."

I walked down the aisles putting in beans, Deb, pasta spirals, tomato sauce, biscuits (not the sweet ones 'cause Mum says they're bad for your teeth), milk, butter, eggs (for omelettes) flour, carrots, peas, peanut butter, jam for Mr E, and bread. I put in some Snickers bars and remembered that I would have to brush my teeth twice as long later. That's what my mum used to say. And ice cream. For Mr E.

Mr E wandered off. I found him behind the front counter where the manager should be, trying to open the cigarette cabinet. It was locked and we couldn't find the key. Mr E found an opened packet on a shelf under the counter. Mum says smoking's bad, makes your teeth go yellow. That's not nice. My dad smoked sometimes, when he wasn't yelling at me.

"Let's go, Mr E. We've got enough food."

Outside, I saw a girl sitting on a seat. She looked upset

'cause she was crying. I walked over slowly and smiled. Mum says that's always the best way to meet new people.

"Hi. I'm Teddy. Are you OK?"

"Have you seen my mum? She told me to wait here for her. That was ages ago. I'm scared she might have forgotten me."

"I've lost my mum too, but you can come home with us if you like. Are you hungry?"

"Yes, and thirsty."

I gave her a can of lemonade and a Snickers bar.

"I've got plenty of food here in the trolley. Do you want to come with us?"

The girl nodded her head.

"What's your name?"

"Isabel, but my friends call me Izzy. I'm nine."

"Hi Izzy. I'm nine too, but I'm going to be ten in two months and fifteen days. We are going to the police station to see if they know where my mum is. Maybe we'll find your mum there?"

Someone had left a motorised wheelchair in the car park. I walked over and pressed the go button. It jerked forward and stopped. It was a good one with a bamboo basket. I learnt once that Pandas eat bamboo. They used to live in China, but now they are all in the zoo. I hope someone is feeding them.

"Hey Mr E. Do you want to ride this home instead of walking?"

He nodded his head. I helped him steer it along the side of the road, around all the empty cars.

We walked home past the police station. The door was open so we walked in. There was a lady sitting there nodding her head. She was wearing a floppy gown that looked like a nighty. It looked dirty and smelled of wee.

"Is that Miriam?" asked Mr E.

"No, Mr E. Remember. She's not here anymore."

"When she's coming back?"

The lady looked up. Her face was all crinkled up, worried-like.

"You're not the police. I'm looking for my wallet. Have you seen it?"

"Hi, I'm Teddy. What's your name?"

"Alice. Alice Cuthbertson. Are you the policeman's son?"

"No, sorry. I'm looking for my mum. Have you seen her?"

"I haven't seen anyone since breakfast. The nurses brought my breakfast and then just disappeared. Have you seen them?"

"No, sorry. We are going home now. Do you want to come with us?"

"Yes, please. But what about my wallet?"

"We'll help you look for it. Don't worry," I said.

I steered Mr E in his wheelchair and pushed the food trolley home. Izzy held Alice's hand. She said it felt rough and wrinkly.

And that is how we survived. The first day.

A BIT LATER

I'm writing all these things down just in case my mum comes back and things go back to normal. I want her to know how we survived. I don't want to forget what happened. My memory is good but I don't remember everything. That's why I like lists. I'll give you a summary so that you will understand how we survived.

1. We started to live together in my house for a few days, but Mr E wanted to go back to his house. He was angry and shouted sometimes because Alice wasn't Miriam.

2. Izzy and me decided to take them to his house. We took them food every day and made sure they had a wash.

3. We had power only when the sun shone. So I cooked rice and pasta and vegetables and Izzy and me took it over to them.

4. The internet worked for a week or so as the satellites must have been working up there in space. Then it stopped too. Before it stopped, I contacted Paul and Johnno two of my internet friends on my Mike Fleming web site. They were teenagers on the spectrum. They said they drove around in abandoned cars until they ran out of petrol. Maybe they'll get caught by the petrol karma man?

5. I could boil water anytime with mum's camping stove. Bunnings (that's a really big shop with lots of batteries and torches and things) had a few full gas bottles. It was over the other side of town, so I had to drive Mr E's wheelchair. That was fun.

6. I taught Izzy how to use the washing machine. We had to wash Alice's sheets a lot because she had something called *incontinence* which I think means *weeing a lot*. We found extra-large nappies at IGA but Alice didn't like them and wouldn't go to sleep.

I found some tablets called melatonin. They worked on Mr E. too.

7. I took the doors and glass windows off mum's car and built a little greenhouse. I got some seeds from Bunnings and grew some vegetables 'cause mum always used to say: *fresh is best.* I hope she won't be cranky when she returns.

8. We'd go for walks a lot 'cause Alice used to wander off looking for her wallet. Izzy and me would take it in turns to go bring her back.

9. We found a house nearby with a lot of chickens running around. Izzy and me caught a few and brought them here. They were very scratchy. They sleep in the garden shed and Izzy looks after them. We get a few eggs every day. I taught Izzy to cook omelettes.

NOW

I wake up with the sun now, or just after. I look on the calendar and see it's eleven months and fifteen days since mum left. Sometimes I feel sad like there is something hard pressing inside my chest where my heart is. But I'm hungry, I have to wash the sheets from next door and I can hear the chickens. Izzy must be collecting the eggs.

"How many today, Izzy?"

"None. Two chickens are gone. I think that fox got them."

I think of a swear word but don't say it. I know there are

guns at the police station but anyhow, I don't like killing things. Mr Todd (the fox) has to eat something.

"I'm going over to see Alice and Mr E. See you later."

I walk over, jump the fence and walk in. I always knock first just in case they are getting dressed. Something's not right. There's a whispering sound coming from Mr E's bedroom. Alice is rocking in a chair next to Mr E's bed. He is asleep, *that's strange*, I think, he's always up early.

"He's gone with the angels," Alice whispers, holding his hand. I don't know what to do. I feel his other hand. It is colder, harder. He is not breathing. He is dead. I know what dead is 'cause I've seen it on *Ozark*.

I gently take Alice's hand and lead her out to the kitchen and make her a cup of tea. Mum always did this when someone was upset. Tea must make people better. While the water is boiling on their camp stove, I try to think what to do. What do you do when someone dies? On *Ozark*, they called the man with a long wagon. Or they tied up the body and put him in the car boot. Or they dug a hole and buried him. I think I'll have to bury Mr E. I look around for anything special that Mr E would like buried with him. On the floor I see an open book that's fallen off the bed. A yellow piece of paper is poking out. I open up the paper and it looks like a letter. Part of it is in strange words I can't understand. But some of it I can read.

Mein liebes Kind,

When you wake you will find me gone. I must go. The Nazis will be searching tomorrow. They have already taken Papa. Mr and Mrs Engel will care for you and

139

raise you as their own. Your name is now Werner. They will look after you. This they have promised. Please do not cry. Learn their holy prayers, one day you may need them. I will always keep a special place open in my heart for you and remember, never forget who you are and that I love you. Always.

Your loving mother, Miriam.

I fold the letter back up and place it inside the book. I thought Mr E would like this buried with him. Some memories are best left this way.

I could feel the pressure tightening inside my chest again. I was holding my breath, and wondering why, almost expecting something to break. I could hear the water boiling. I went and got Izzy. She'd have to look after Alice while I dug the hole for Mr E and stop her walking off. I didn't feel like talking, especially while I was digging. I was saying to myself, inside my head: *I just wanna freeze up and die, right now.* But I couldn't, I had to bury Mr E.

The ground was cold and hard. Mr E's shovel was old and rusted. It took me most of the day digging. I stopped to eat when the hole was as deep as my knees.

I kept digging.

Later in the afternoon, the top of the hole was level with my shoulders. I figured that was probably deep enough.

"Have you ever seen someone buried?" I asked Izzy.

"Only once on TV," she said.

"I think they say a prayer or make a speech," I said. So I said something nice about Mr E.

"Mr Engelman was a nice man. He was my friend. He loved Miriam like I love my mum. Mr E loved his roses, they reminded him of her. I'll take care of your roses now, I promise."

That's about all I could think of to say.

We moved his body gently from his bed into the wheelchair. We pushed him outside into the garden and stood for a minute before the roses, not saying anything. Alice was rocking back and forth so Izzy held her hand. We tried to lift Mr E into the hole but the wheelchair toppled over and he just fell in. "Sorry, Mr E," I whispered.

I placed his book and letter on his chest and his hands on top of the book. Like in *Ozark*. He would have wanted that. I don't know why, it just felt right. Then we covered him with the soil. Later, I'd plant roses on top, but not now.

That night, after putting Alice to bed, Izzy and I sat outside under the stars. I showed her where the Southern Cross was and one of the pointer stars called *Alpha Centauri*.

"You know Aboriginal people could always find their way around at night by the stars."

"How far away are they?" she asked.

"*Alpha Centauri* is the closest. It's four point five light years away. If you were light, it would take you that long to get there."

"I'd like to go there one day. What would it be like?" she asked.

She held my hand while I thought of something to say. What would Gumbo say, if he could talk? But he was asleep, under my pillow. I couldn't think of anything. All I could feel was something warm inside, and the hard feeling around my heart, melting away.

Containment

Olivia Hamilton

Was chewing on favourite slipper—the one kept hidden in garden, the one Mum Two-leg don't know I stole—when heard crash, then grunting-shuffling sound behind compost bin. It was mid of day, Mum at work, so I protecting. But I was asleep on grass, sun warming fur, and didn't want to move for no reason. So sent nose up into air. Sniffed. Dog smell. Sent ears to east-north-east. Listened. Shuffle, snuffle, grunt. Sighing, for didn't want to leave sun-grass, thought better to be safe than sorry like Mum Two-leg always says, and stretched the way to standing. First bowed thanks to grass for soft place to rest, then shook head at sun to say back soon old friend, and trotted over to bin.

Strange thing greeted me when I arrived. On other side, between bin and fence, sat creature same smell as dog, but not dog. Different sound, different shape. I trembled in hind legs but dug in claws, bared teeth, growled. Garden belong to me; house belong to Mum Two-leg. My job to protect.

"Woof," I said. "Woof-woof-woof!"

"Well of course there'd be a dog here," creature said. "Is there anything else that could go wrong today?"

"Woo-oof grrr," I said.

Strange creature made sound like laugh but no joy in it. Then stood on two legs, shuffled around compost, wiped bit of carrot skin and dirt off nose. Must be creature was hungry-lost, not have no house nor garden for own self. Creature moved into light of sun. Transforming while walked. Went from looking like dog walking on hind legs to full-grown two-leg. Naked, pink like Mum Two-leg when go in wet room every morn of day.

Creature shook herself, looked down at hands and feet.

"I don't think I'll ever get used to this," said in sad voice. Tried to cover naked body with hands.

"Whm mmh www," I whimpered. Lied down, covered head with paws. Never in all my days thought would see dog become two-leg before my own eyes. How came creature to have this happen? "Wooo?" I asked. Hoped creature still spoke dog.

"It's a long story, friend, and in this form, I'm afraid to say, I feel embarrassed by my skin. It is a curse to live like a two-leg." Voice of creature soft, sad still, like not sure of place in world.

Creature looked towards house, start to move. But I still guarding. "Grrr."

Creature stopped. Looked down. Sighed. "I understand."

Creature turned and walked to fence, looked over from where came, into back lane were Mum Two-leg and me sometimes walk. Empty. But creature seemed afraid all right. After peered over, she crouched down low to ground, hanged head between knees. Seemed trying to make herself small as could be.

I trotted over, licked her hand, like sometimes did for Mum Two-leg when sad thoughts crowded. Always helped her. Thought maybe would help strange creature too.

Head down, creature started to talk low.

"You've heard of werewolves, I suppose?"

I lay down low, covered head with paws.

"Yes, that's them," said creature. "As it turns out, the virus has evolved; now, it's not only two-legs who can be infected."

Lifted paw off one eye. "Woooo-th-fff?"

"It was a surprise to me too, when I found out, believe me."

Creature breathed deep, leaned back against fence. I put head on creature's knee. Listening.

"They attacked at midnight, like they always do. My Mum and Dad had been fighting, and Sister Two-leg was upset. She packed a bag and snuck down the stairs. When she opened the door, I slipped out behind her. You know as well as I do that two-legs don't pay enough attention to the Moon. I don't think she even knew what kind of danger she was in. And it was my job to protect her. But I—but…"

Creature breathed hard, tears dripping from her eyes. I looked up, licked salt off cheeks. Felt hand on head, fingers stroking ears. Bliss.

"As soon as we left the house, I felt a shiver travel through my whole body. Moon was shining brightly in the clear sky. I could hear the werewolves howling. Sister ignored them. Just kept on walking. I could smell the stench of them getting closer. I nipped at her hand, butted my head against her legs, tried to get her to turn away. But it was too late. A big shape sped towards us, fangs glittering white in the moonlight. He leapt at Sister. I jumped in front of her, trying to protect her, but it was no fair match. I got one small scratch in before his jaws latched onto my leg. He tossed me aside like I weighed nothing. I lay there, bleeding, watching the horrible beast drag my sister away, and I thought I was going to die. But in the morning, when the sun came up, I felt myself start to change. I turned into a two-leg. I felt all these new emotions, things

I'd never felt before. Like shame. I managed to find a house with no dog to protect it, and stole some clothing hanging in the backyard. I walked for what seemed like hours, looking for any sign of the werewolf's den. Then, when the sun set, I found myself starting to transform back into a dog. And it's been that way ever since. It feels like I'm splitting in two, trying to live two lives. I don't know how much longer I can cope."

Creature still smelt sad, but no tears, only short shallow breaths and body still and heavy. No more patting head. I moved closer, placed paws on creature's chest, licked all over face. After a bit, creature started to laugh. Happy again.

Then remembered. Still I not know how came creature to be in Garden. "Rrr, grrr wufff. Rruf?"

Creature silent. Still. Scared.

"Rrrufff?" I said again. Needed to know.

"Two nights ago, I finally located the werewolf den. It was abandoned, but I caught the faint trace of Sister's scent. I followed it deep into the cavern and through a narrow tunnel. Eventually, I saw the faint glow of lights and heard muttered two-leg voices. I crept up to the edge of the tunnel, nuzzle close to the ground, and sniffed. Sweat, fear. I looked up and saw that the tunnel opened into a room deep underground. There were cages in the room, and in the cages, two-legs. Dirty, sweaty two-legs, with tubes coming out of their arms. Sister was one of them, and a big man, might have been the werewolf that bit me. There was another two-leg, wearing a white coat and face mask, walking around between the cages, watching. I realised that the sun must be nearing its zenith somewhere up above us, because I started to transform. The two-leg heard me. He came after me, yelling for back-up. I ran. Somehow, I still can't believe how, I made it outside and escaped. So far,

I've managed to avoid being taken, but they got close today. Oh dog, what's going to happen if they catch me?"

Creature again sad, buried face in my fur and cried. I not knowing what to think. Not used to think for future, only sun, and grass, and Mum Two-leg pats, and food, and sometimes run-and-catch in park.

All of sudden, back lane was full of snarling-growling-hissing-cawing. Could hear dogs, cats, birds, every which thing. Neighbourhood watch. Creature and me shivered both together. Looked through gap in fence, saw one two-leg, then another, big masks on faces. Moving slow, searching. Saw first one lift gun, aim.

"Run!" whispered creature.

No need to tell I twice. Crouched low, we ran towards house. Crawled under, into dark space between floor and dirt. Good hiding place. Kept crawling, hoped creature would follow. Front side of house maybe clear of two-legs, I hoped. Dirt under house dry and bothersome, not living like garden. Felt sneeze coming but held it. Was almost to front, creature not far behind.

Heard voice calling in garden.

"I've got eyes on 'em!"

Gunshot loud, kicked up dirt beside creature. Scrambled faster to get to front of house. Hoped enough time to run. Then, face covered by mask bent low to ground in front of us. I snarled, bared teeth, as hand reached in. Creature beside me snarled too. More hands reaching. In struggle, felt creature's small human teeth bite my back leg. Hands pulled us out into light at front of house.

"Gotcha," said two-leg. "And who's your friend?"

Heard creature cry out in pain. Saw two-leg lift hand,

147

holding needle. Snarled, twisted, but no use. World went black.

When awoke, saw I was in a cage in big cavern, like underground. One light shone, cast shadows all over. Tried to move but heavy feeling. Whimpered.

"The dog's awake, Doc," said voice somewhere near.

Two-leg in white coat knelt in front of cage. "There, there, boy, it's OK," he said.

I not trusting. Not felt OK. But two-leg kept talking.

"We're just keeping you under observation. The virus is mutating every day. Need to make sure we keep everyone—every dog, too—who might have been infected contained. It's about the safety of the masses. You understand."

I not understand.

Days passed, and nights, all same. Only could tell time since creatures all around changing every night or day, some from two-leg to werewolf, some from dog to two-leg. Doc two-leg come and go, bringing more werewolves. Soon needed more cages. Room full to bursting. I still not changed, but Doc not caring. Said all of us had to stay, we under his obser-vation. Long word. I worried about Mum, missed her pats. Whined and howled and whimpered all of one whole week. Not changed a thing. Still stuck in cage, still visit by Doc, still waiting. But for what?

Tried, but couldn't find creature in all full cages. Must be was on other side of cavern.

Sometime, more two-legs in white coats came. Carried needles. Waited till all creatures in half-way between dog and two-leg, then jabbed them. Since I not transforming, I not given needle. Doc decided I safe. If safe all this time, why still in cage? Still. When all creatures jabbed and stopped transforming, cages opened, all ran out happy through tunnel.

I joined, smelled freedom. Outside, blinked at sun, bowed to grass. Found Mum Two-leg waiting. Wagged tail, jumped, licked, rolled on back, big smile.

In crowd, smelled creature. Was happy, tail wagging, held in arms of girl what must be missing Sister. Looked lovely dog. Could be friends, if met in park. Before could say goodbye, Mum Two-leg pats distracted. Bliss.

Went home. House was same as before. Ran into garden, lay in sun. Night, sat on couch with mum. Dreamed of creature. Dreamed we running in park together, rolling on grass, digging in dirt.

Next day, Mum Two-leg at work. At midday, felt tingle in legs, then a shiver in my chest. I tried to bark, but it sounded different. I felt pain as my body changed. What was happening? I looked down, saw hands where my paws should be, naked skin where once was fur. For the first time in my life, I felt shame.

The Monsignor

Graham Davidson

The full moon highlighted the age etched into Monsignor O'Grady's face as he wrapped his grey woollen scarf tighter around his neck. He approached the Coach House Inn, steam spreading from his lips each time he exhaled.

The MacManus brothers sat at a makeshift table; two empty barrels with an old door laid across the top. Two other men sat across from them. A modest fire burned in a butchered forty-four-gallon drum next to the table. Its red coals and dancing flames created a warm glow that illuminated the brothers' faces.

The priest placed his bag on the table next to a half full bottle of Highlander Scotch whisky then extended his gloved hands to warm them over the fire. He scanned the table with a distrustful glare then addressed the brothers. "Is this the last of your patrons?"

His eyes betrayed his envy of how warm his hosts appeared as they sat in loose fitting shirts and waistcoats. They were listening to the cricket broadcast through the partially open window to the public bar where a Bakelite radio held pride of place on the mantelpiece.

John MacManus raised a hand up toward the priest, signalling his wish for the conversation to hold until an appropriate break in the broadcast.

Benaud comes around the wicket for the last ball of his

over and May slips it through the covers for one run.

The men looked to each other, gave a half nod, then John turned back to the priest, signalling an opportunity to talk before the next over commenced. He leaned back in his rickety chair, pushing his foot against one of the barrels so the chair supported his weight on two legs. His brother, Patrick, seemed oblivious to the priest's presence. He was preoccupied with how many smoke rings he could produce from a single drag on his cigarette. The other two men were content to sit in silence.

John's Irish accent was unmistakable. "Aye, the last of them would've left a good hour ago."

"What about these two?"

"Well, Your Holiness, seeing the Ashes are on tonight, and neither Jimmy nor George here have the means to own a radio of their own, we figured the Christian thing to do would be to set ourselves up with this table for the evening and enjoy a whisky or two while you go about your business and Benaud's boys take it to the Poms."

The priest made his best effort to look intimidating. "Hmmph! And what of the guest rooms? Has everyone retired for the night?"

John let the chair fall back on four legs, then poured himself a generous scotch. He didn't look up as he replied, "I don't rightly see that's any of your business." He sipped on his drink then turned to Monsignor O'Grady. "We don't make it our business to pay much heed to the comings and goings of our guests. And you know what? It's only because of the Mayor's request, when he came here accompanied by the widow Jenkins and the local constabulary, that we were willing to call last drinks early this evening."

Furrows appeared in his brow as he glared at the priest.

"And it's all for the sake of some hare-brained scheme on your part that you can make that woman feel comfortable when she chooses to sit at the back of the dining room…supposedly trying to be discreet when she's having dinner with the Mayor whenever his missus is out of town."

The cricket commentators discussing the state of the pitch at Old Trafford filled the uneasy quiet that followed John's accusation.

If the Australians are to have any hope, they need the ball to start turning more, and I can't see that happening on this pitch.

The priest took a handkerchief from his pocket and mopped beads of sweat from his brow that had formed while he stood by the fire in his overcoat and scarf. He coughed in an unconscious effort to mask his anxiety, then rubbed at the white stubble on his chin. He took a deep breath and raised a trembling finger to the brothers. "I might remind you both that it's not by personal choice that I'm here this evening. I'm here to perform God's work."

Patrick flicked the ash from the end of his cigarette into the old tin he used as an ashtray. He stared at the stars rather than look the priest in the eye. "We never asked you to come here. You've caused us considerable cost and inconvenience with your fearmongering about town."

The Monsignor's lower lip quivered as he continued waving his finger. "I'll have you know, Patrick MacManus, no fewer than three parishioners have come to me saying they've been disturbed by a sense of evil in the back of that dining room."

Patrick watched the smoke rise from his cigarette then dissipate into the night sky. "And in the meantime, another fifty or so people have sat at the same table and had a great time of it. It's not our fault if people who have their own demons want to blame their problems on some superstitious nonsense that there's some sort of evil lurking in our premises."

John lifted an elbow to the table and rested his chin in the palm of his hand. He cast a glance toward the priest. "The fact is, Your Holiness, this old building has a mind of its own. If it doesn't like someone, it lets them know. Seems to me like it's doing us a favour...discouraging the riff raff and the more fucked up of our patrons. I can't see that's likely to change because you decide to go in there and fling a bit of holy water around while saying a few prayers and the like. I'd just appreciate it if you can do whatever it is you want to do and be on your way so we can enjoy the rest of the cricket broadcast in peace."

"I'll have you know one of those three parishioners was—"

John finished the sentence for him, "—the Mayor himself. And that, Your Holiness, is the only reason Pat and I are letting you play your little game. It'd be good if you can be getting in there and doing your thing. We're only out here in the cold night air because you requested privacy as you go about your business. We'd all much rather be sitting in the comfort of the Public Bar by the radio." He paused for a moment then asked, "Why'd you insist on us being out here rather than in there anyway?"

Patrick stared straight ahead. Cynicism dripped off his every word. "I reckon he's never done this before, and he's scared that he'll look like he doesn't know what he's doing."

"Hmmph!" The priest turned away from the MacManus brothers. He took his leather bag from the table and shuffled into the sandstone building.

Patrick poured himself a drink. "How long do you reckon,

mate?"

"Hmm. I reckon he'll be going in, sprinkling some holy water around and mumbling a few prayers. Then he'll be running off to the Mayor bragging about how he's sent the devil packing. Ten minutes, max."

The two men across the table nodded in agreement.

Patrick replied, "Are you sure about that?" He took a deep drag on his cigarette, then, after exhaling, replied to his own question. "I reckon he's going to be poking a hornets' nest in there. I can't see the place taking too kindly to his attitude."

"Well, I guess we'll soon be finding out."

*

Monsignor O'Grady closed the large French door behind him as he entered the Inn. He removed his overcoat and scarf, hanging them on the hallstand just inside the door. There was a myriad of reasons he'd come up with to deter others who'd asked him to perform this manner of ritual in the past, and he had no intention of letting the MacManus boys know how close they were to the truth. In more than half a century as a priest, this was the first time he'd agreed to attempt ridding a building of evil...to perform an exorcism. It was a word that didn't sit kindly with him or what he believed in.

It felt so ironic.

As the years had rolled by, he'd found himself questioning his faith at every turn. And the more his faith drained away, the more he compensated by throwing himself ever deeper into his job with what others perceived as evangelical zeal. He felt like an actor whose talents would never be truly appreciated for what they were. There was a kind of solace in how those who held faith looked to him as a beacon of hope.

He walked past the entrance to the public bar and into the lounge area that served as a buffer before the dining room. As soon as he entered the room, he felt a chill that took him by surprise considering that flames continued to flicker in the fireplace.

The sound of the cricket broadcast coming from the public bar created a surreal backdrop to his passage through the dimly lit building.

He stopped.

Was that the sound of someone placing a glass on a table?

He turned and stared into the darkness at the far end of the room.

"Hello? Who's there?"

There was a moment's silence before an articulate voice replied from the shadows, "Why are you doing this?"

The priest lifted his free hand above his eyes, as though it might increase the visibility. "Who are you? And what are you doing here?"

"Who am I? That's of no concern. As for why I'm here, let's just say that I'm talking to you now because I believe it's in everyone's best interest, particularly your own, if you turn around and leave now. Or perhaps you might prefer to join me for a drink before you leave, so you can say you took your time to go about your work."

Monsignor O'Grady took a step toward the dark corner. A floorboard creaked underfoot. The only other sound came from the crackling fire and the cricket broadcast in the next room.

Archer bowls to Sheppard and he puts it through the slips for what should be another two runs, leaving him just two shy of his century.

The priest stopped and straightened his back in an effort to appear taller. Being unable to see the man in the shadows, he was unsure exactly where he should look. "I'm here to do God's work."

"Oh, come on, Monsignor. You and I both know you don't believe that. You're only here to appease the Mayor and that widow you're so fond of—"

"Why are you still here anyway? And who are you? The MacManus boys assured me the bars were empty."

"So many questions. I am here because, like many others, I have little choice in the matter. Who I am is of no consequence, and I doubt that you'd believe me anyway. As for the MacManus boys, they spoke the truth."

The priest furrowed his brow as his agitation became palpable. "You speak in riddles rather than having the common decency to give straight answers to straight questions."

"I doubt you'll see it that way when you look back on our conversation later."

"How is it you know who I am, and what my purpose is?"

"I listen."

"You questioned my faith."

"I'm a good judge of character."

Seeing they were the only ones in the room, the priest chose not to debate the issue. "Why is it that you don't want me to go about my work?"

"Because, to a degree, the widow, mayor, and constable are right. There is a presence residing in the back wall of the dining room. But to call it evil isn't quite accurate. It responds to the emotional wellbeing of those in its direct vicinity. It has occupied this space longer than this building has stood here."

"What a load of codswallop!"

"Call it what you will, but it's very real, and there are many who have gone to a great deal of effort to keep it calm and contained within the comfort of the lathe and plaster of the back wall."

"Are you telling me there's a spirit that lives within the wall?"

"'Spirit' is not a term I'd use. Are you familiar with what science has learned about the workings of the brain, and how this mass of chemical reactions and electrical conductivity plays host to the mind?"

"You know that what you are saying borders on blasphemy?"

"Oh good, so you do understand. The thing is, sometimes part or all of a consciousness might spill out of its host and be absorbed by an organic structure that has enough similar qualities. Over time, it may even get passed from one conductor to another."

The priest remained silent as he tried to comprehend exactly what his companion was saying.

"The horsehair used to bind the plaster together in these walls makes them an excellent conductor. When this building was constructed, the back wall of the dining room absorbed something that had dwelt within the ground for thousands of years. And that has taught the walls to absorb other such leftovers as they've come along." There was a brief pause. "Like myself."

Feeling the coldness in the room had dissipated, the priest approached the table in the corner. As he drew closer his eyes adjusted to the shadows. The table appeared to be empty. He turned around and saw there was a light switch by the door. He rushed across and flicked on the switch, confirming he was alone in the room; just him and the sound of the cricket broadcast.

I've got to say, Richie Benaud looks a little lost for what he needs to do here...

*

Monsignor O'Grady entered the dining room and placed his bag on a table. He pulled out a simple purple vestment with gold trim and a cross at either end then hung it from his neck before laying out his bible, holy water, and incense. The Lord's Prayer issued from his lips as he prepared, not by design, but as a means of distraction. There had been somebody in the lounge and, having not wanted their identity to be known, they must have slipped out through the kitchen when he approached. Nothing else made sense. The MacManus boys were known for their love of pranks and practical jokes, and he'd be taking them to task over this one on his departure.

Within the plaster on the back wall, the horsehair was tingling. There was someone close by who was having a discernible negative impact on the space. One by one, each strand of hair within the lathe and plaster woke and found itself drawn to the same sensation. They worked together to coax the negativity forward, so it might be explored and understood.

For the first time since entering the building, the priest noticed steam on his breath when he exhaled. It drew his attention to how it seemed to be getting colder since he'd entered the room. He looked at the last of the smouldering coals in the fireplace that dominated the middle of the back wall and put it down to the fact that it was no longer producing heat. He found himself compelled to move toward the part of the wall that was to the right of the fireplace, feeling the sense one feels when being watched. Yet this was more intense. He felt like he was being examined. His eyes darted to either side of the room, trying to avoid that part of the wall he was approaching. *I don't want to look at it. I can't. I won't.*

His eyes made contact with that part of the wall, and he saw in it an abyss.

The pulsing sensations running through the horsehair within the wall felt the energy of the priest's rising fear as it pulled him closer. Now it could learn more fully about him and his intentions. As the connection grew stronger and the sentience in the wall feasted on the emotional angst, it reached out to ask questions.

The priest put his hand against the wall then thought to himself: *What am I doing? It's just a wall. Nothing more, nothing less.* With a jolt, he pulled himself away and retreated to his bag. Not knowing what else to do, he started performing what he thought an exorcism ritual might consist of. His fumbling with the incense belied his sense of ill ease. On trying to light it, he broke the first match, then the second one went out. *Look inside yourself, old man.* He continued reciting the Lord's Prayer in a muted whisper as he lit the third match and held it to the block of incense until it started burning, then closed the brass cover of the burner and started swinging it from its ornate chain toward the back wall. *What have you ever done of value?*

Monsignor O'Grady closed his eyes as he continued swinging the incense and reciting his prayer, hoping the question would pass like so many ill thoughts do when ignored. But it didn't work. The question grew louder until he felt compelled to answer. He opened his eyes and bellowed at the wall, "I'm here to banish you!"

Banishment?

He looked in horror at the wall as it revealed the abyss to him once more.

This time it was clearer.

This time he understood.

The abyss wasn't in the wall. The wall was showing him a reflection. The abyss was inside him. His life and his soul, everything that made him was empty and meaningless. He had nothing to offer but lies and deceit. His pretence of altruism and goodwill was a hollow veneer that hid an emptiness so vast he felt himself standing on a precipice of falsehoods that was falling away beneath his feet.

How dare you enter my domain harbouring thoughts that you might tell others you facilitated my departure.

Monsignor O'Grady fell headlong into the darkness, the wall's accusations reverberating through his head as he plummeted deep into the eternal nothingness of his self.

I would draw from you something for myself, but there is nothing to take. Leave me. Go and live your pitiful lie.

The priest's eyes opened, and he saw the room spin. He felt a weakness in his knees and stumbled, then used the tables to support himself as he reached for the holy water. Despite his lack of faith, he couldn't think of anything else to do. His hand trembled as he waved his brass wand of water that, as always, he hadn't bothered to bless. "In the name of the Lord Jesus Christ, I compel you to leave this place!"

Nothing.

The priest repeated, "I compel you to leave!"

I've had enough…time for you to leave.

He felt as though he were being pushed, not physically,

but mentally. In his mind, the wall was growing...and it was angry. Seeing again the reflection of his own emptiness, he threw his things into his bag and grabbed it without bothering to properly close it. He felt like a storm was swirling within his head as he struggled toward the dining room door before the wall could swallow him in the horror of his own reality. On having made it through to the lounge he fell to the floor, the door to the dining room slamming shut behind him. Had he pulled it shut himself, or had it been closed by whatever had sent him from the room? He didn't know and didn't care. He sat with his head in his hands and sobbed uncontrollably.

He had no idea how long he'd been sitting there when he was brought back to his senses by the men outside cheering in response to the cricket broadcast. Somehow the radio seemed louder than before as the commentator declared: *And he's out! May is out for forty-three runs after a brilliant ball from Benaud.*

*

The men were laughing and joking about Richie Benaud's good fortune when John looked over his shoulder and saw the look of terror etched into the priest's face as he took tentative steps toward the table with his bag clutched to his breast. John asked, "Would you be in need a little Scotch whisky to calm your nerves?"

The priest gave a barely perceptible nod as he continued toward the table. Once there, he dropped his bag and fell to the ground, trembling and speechless. Patrick stared straight ahead and said, "I told you he was poking at a hornets' nest."

John glared at his brother. "That may be so, but now's not

the time for 'I told you so's.'" He got out of his chair and helped the priest up. "Come on, Your Holiness, we've got a spare pew for you here by the fire." He poured the priest a generous portion of scotch. "I felt pretty sure you'd be needing a wee drop once you came out, so I took the liberty of making sure we were prepared."

The priest's hand shook so much as he raised the glass that some of the whisky spilled over the side. He took a tentative sip at first, then drank the rest as though it were water.

John returned to his seat, poured the priest another shot, then asked, "So, what happened?"

The priest's face was blank as he replied, "I...I don't rightly know."

One of the men, an indigenous man called Jimmy with a smile that lit up his face in such a way that it was generally contagious, put a hand on the Priest's shoulder and asked, "Did you meet the squatter on your way in?"

It was only then that the priest remembered his conversation in the lounge bar. He turned to Jimmy and said, "I can't see that's funny, as far as pranks go."

Jimmy slapped him on the back. "Son of a gun...you did get to meet him! Did he say anything to you?"

The priest looked around the table. "Which one of you was responsible for that!" He started shaking again as he continued in a softer voice, "That's a cruel trick to play on someone when you obviously knew what I was walking into."

John leaned across the table and said, "Your Holiness, I promise you, you were the only living being in there tonight. We've all encountered the squatter at one time or another, but he's not real."

"I spoke to a man in there for a good five minutes. He knew

everything about me and why I was there."

Jimmy's friend, George, spoke for the first time. "That sounds like the squatter alright."

The priest asked, "So, does this squatter have a name?"

John replied, "No doubt he did once, but no one knows it now. You're one of the lucky ones if he spoke to you for a whole five minutes. He's never spoken a word to me."

Jimmy said, "He talks to people when they're about to face a crisis and he gives them a bit of advice."

George followed up. "Mostly, people just feel him in there when they're feeling down and lonely."

The priest asked, "Have any of you spoken to him?"

Patrick replied, "He started up a conversation with me once, but I told him to fuck off."

John glared at his brother. "God but you're full of shit." He turned to the priest. "None of us have spoken directly with him, but we all know people who have." He leaned in closer to the priest. "But what I'm more interested in is…what happened in the dining room?"

"I…I really don't want to…"

"We're all aware of a darkness that dwells in that wall, but it only ever comes out when people who are fucked up in one way or another sit right up next to it. And for some reason, those people, when they come in, are always drawn to that particular spot."

The priest sat in silence and poured himself another drink.

Patrick asked, "What'll you be telling the Mayor?"

"I'm going to tell him that I cleansed the place in God's name, but that it's probably still better if he, and the others who had troubles here, don't return."

Patrick replied, "I think that's the first sensible thing you've said all night."

John stood up and said, "I'll get your coat and scarf from inside, else you'll likely get a chill on your way back to the rectory."

The priest's eyes looked humble as he looked up at John, "Thank you, they're just inside the door."

John strode toward the door, then froze. He turned around and said, "Pat, Jimmy, I think you might want to come and check this out. It doesn't feel good."

John took a tentative step inside, just enough so he could reach the coat and scarf that hung from a hook on the hallstand. He retrieved them as the other men reached the door.

The three men stared wide-eyed into the darkness as Patrick said, "Holy shit. I'll be fucked if I'm going in there."

John replied, "It's the worst it's been as far as I can remember."

Jimmy asked, "Want me to go and get Aunty Melba?"

John replied, "Aye." He rummaged in his pocket and pulled out a set of keys then handed them to Jimmy. "Here, you can take the Morrie."

*

First light was breaking when Jimmy pulled up out the front with Aunty Melba in the passenger seat. The cricket being over now, George had already headed off for home. As Jimmy got out of the green Morris Minor, John called out, "Perfect timing, we just finished the last of the Scotch, and I'll feel more comfortable going inside for another after Aunty's done her thing."

Aunty Melba got out of the car. She was a rotund indigenous

woman with long grey hair tied up in a loose bun. A touch of a waddle in her short stride betrayed the painful arthritis in her knees and her broad smile revealed that, despite her age, she still had almost a full set of teeth. Jimmy fetched a tin bucket from the boot. It contained some eucalyptus leaves, paperbark, stringybark, and some type of weed that he wasn't familiar with. He handed Aunty Melba the bucket and she approached the brothers shaking her head. "It's little wonder you got a problem here now, letting that priest fella go in there and set out to anger them spirits."

Patrick paid little attention to the conversation, content to focus on the cigarette he was rolling. John stood up and said, "It's good to see you too, Aunty. To be honest, we really weren't given much say in the matter. But I can tell you one thing for sure, we're not likely to be seeing the Monsignor again any time soon."

She ignored him and turned to look toward the building. "It been a good twenty years since I've done come here and calmed this poor migaloo." Aunty Melba walked up to the door and put her hands on her hips as she spoke to the building. "What are you mad about? The white fella priest ran off, and you're still here." She pulled a box of matches from her pocket, stuck one, and then grabbed a buddle from the bucket at her feet. She lit it and started waving it in front of her, a trail of smoke following the path of her arm. "Aunty Melba's gonna help you relax and get some sleep." She picked up the bucket in her free hand and walked into the building.

One Night

J. A. Haigh

Elki swayed from foot to foot, clutching her yellow backpack. As the car pulled away from the curb, she saw the pale flash of her mother's hand, a token, guilty wave before she vanished from sight.

Elki didn't wave back.

*

"Can't you just tell them you can't work tonight? What about the others?"

"Elki," Mum had cried, "I can't just pick and choose. You'll be fine, it's only for one night. Olwen is a lovely, kind lady and she's doing us a huge favour. I expect you to be on your absolute, best behaviour. Do you hear me?"

"You can't really expect me to stay overnight in that house. Rats will probably chew off half my face while I'm asleep. How will you feel then?"

"Relieved? For God's sake, Elki. Don't be such a drama queen."

*

The house was a dump. Lumber, scrap iron, broken pots and weeds crowded the yard, while scrappy-looking chickens and cats wound through the heaps of junk.

'Olwen' was an icon of the street. The wicked witch of Westfield. She wore black, always. Black dress. Black shoes. Black stockings. Black apron. Always.

It's only for one night, Elki reminded herself. Plastering a smile on her face, she stomped up the steps.

Gruff but welcoming, Olwen ushered her into a bedroom stacked waist-high with aging cookery magazines. Bags of wool and super-kitsch knick-knacks littered every bare surface. The bedspread was a nauseating orange.

Dinner was salty chicken casserole with beans, served on tray-tables in front of Millionaire Hotseat, the overhead light switched off.

Olwen sneered. "Eddie McGuire. Awful man." Her pasty skin showed a deeper pigment in the shadows, bouncing back warm reflections from the TV.

It was a relief when bedtime came.

Elki woke to the sharp squeak of a chair on linoleum. Moonlight shone through the lace curtains. Tied at her wrist, a thread of black ribbon. She plucked at it, puzzled.

From the kitchen doorway, a dim light showed, and, under the lingering whiff of casserole, an odour to the air, like the musty scent of blood and bone.

Scattered across the formica table was a handful of knuckle bones.

At the lone seat, Olwen tugged something from under her woollen robe. A bird? A dead rat? And tossed it—a dull splash—into a soup tureen, before clattering the ceramic lid back into place.

The old woman tapped the dish twice with a wooden spoon

and something rattled back from within. On her wrist, a black ribbon matching Elki's.

Elki stared as Olwen's ancient face shifted, drifting like a photo under water, the skin and bones melting, reforming, resolving into a passable image of Elki's own face.

The witch looked up.

*

Mum arrived early next morning to take her home.

"Not so bad?"

"What a complete nightmare," snapped Elki as she climbed into the car.

"Oh, for God's sake, Elki, it was one night," exclaimed Mum. "Don't be such a drama queen."

*

Inside the dark house, Olwen wailed.

Prudence

Peter Mark Lewis

A vehicle came into sight and Prudence brightened with anticipation. Was this the one? Was this HER bus at long last? She avoided looking at its destination display, preferring the suspense of not knowing, the delicious mystery of the lucky dip rather than the opening of the retrieved package.

Fellow travellers around her stirred even though it was still some distance away. An old woman, who had been waiting at the bus stop longer than anybody, took off her glasses and cleaned them with a faded handkerchief, her fingers moving with ritual deliberation like bony puppets in a well-rehearsed ballet. Then she returned her glasses to the indents on her nose and squinted at the vehicle's destination display and announced, "*Opportunity!*"

Several travellers became excited. Magazines and phones were stowed, followed by a rustle of money from wallets and purses. This was a bus that did not come very often, if at all. For a moment it looked like everybody was going to climb on board at once. Some faces switched from joy to sullen resentment, as if they had found a winning lottery ticket but had to share it. Angry glances were exchanged as a queue formed next to the bus pole.

Prudence, however, had anticipated this situation and managed to position herself at the front, so she was well-placed to see the destination details on the bus as it drew closer.

"*Opportunity*—via *Getrichquickscheme*."

Her enthusiasm faded. She had been there before. It was like Vegas; fun and exciting but too much of a gamble. Not to be deterred, she kept her position as the bus rolled to a stop in front of the queue.

Opportunity knocked as it shut down. It was a gleaming well-oiled machine, imposing yet strangely tatty when viewed up close. The driver—a leonine man with an expensive moustache and a cheap suit—bounded from his seat, threw open the doors with a wide flourish and boomed, "Welcome to the Opportunity Express!"

The travellers parted before him like the Red Sea and returned his hungry smile with shy grins of their own. This was their lucky day!

Or was it, thought Prudence to herself. She gave a polite little cough as if to announce herself then spoke in a quiet voice.

"Very nice of you to pick us up, Mr…"

"Deals!" he bellowed, as if speaking to a deaf person, "Shade E. Deals…but my friends call me Shady." He winked to his captive audience and they responded with a titter of amusement. Prudence, however, merely smiled and continued.

"So, Mr Deals, you're taking us to *Opportunity* via *Getrichquickscheme*."

"Yes, my dear," replied Shady with slick warmth. "That's the fastest way."

"I see," said Prudence, raising an eyebrow. "Does that involve any short cuts?"

Shady's grin widened into an array of predatory gold-capped teeth.

"Well, my dear…"

"Prudence."

"My dear Prudence," he continued, "of course we have to take some liberties along the way. If we were to follow the conventional route we might never get anywhere." He finished the comment with another wink to the audience, this time more conspiratorial. Once again there was a mirthful response.

"I see," said Prudence with an innocent expression. "So, you occasionally veer from the straight and narrow then?"

Shady waved a ring-decorated hand as if brushing away an annoying fly.

"I'd hardly put it that way, my dear. I don't do anything to endanger my clients."

"But you do drive a *Hardbargain*," she said, patting the bullnose of the bus.

"Er, yes…and very comfortable it is too." A bead of sweat began to run down his forehead.

"For the person in charge," she added, indicating his luxurious leather chair. "But aren't the passenger seats made of cheap plastic?"

Shady harrumphed. "High quality *Bumsride* polycarbonate if you don't mind. Made in China to fit smart-arses such as yourself."

Prudence merely smiled at the insult and continued. "If you're going via *Getrichquickscheme*, doesn't that mean you have to use the *Tax bypass*?"

"Um, possibly…" replied Shady. His leonine countenance pained as if he had reached for a rose but got a thorn in his paw instead.

"Well," added Prudence with quiet deliberation, "if that's the case then you and your passengers could get lost in *Dodgeypaperwork*, couldn't you? Worse, you might go to

Loseyourshirt. Perhaps even wind up in *Liquidation*."

There was a muted gasp from some of the people around them.

"Madam," interrupted Shady, defensive. "Are you implying I'd lead my passengers astray?"

"Merely stating the obvious, Mr Deals."

"Well, my dear *Prudence*," he replied with sarcastic vengeance, "Perhaps I can be *obvious* then and ask you to step out of the way of less difficult passengers."

With that he pushed her aside. A stampede of enthusiastic participants jostled past; their eyes gleaming as they thrust money into Shady's sweaty palms. In less than a minute his hands and pockets were full, and he gave Prudence a smug sneer of victory as he slammed the door in her face and returned to his seat. *Opportunity* knocked again as it shuddered to life, and a large gout of smoke poured out the back as it moved away, leaving behind the distinct smell of burning money.

Prudence glanced toward the old woman, who had never even roused herself from the benches let alone join the queue, and their eyes shared a moment of smug amusement. Not everybody had climbed aboard the bus, but the crowd was noticeably thinner.

Another bus came into view. This one did not generate any anticipation however, not even with Prudence, nor did it have an air of mystery.

Predictability—via *Tediousrepetition*.

The pallid driver made no attempt to invite people onboard, other than open the door, but a surprising number of passengers entered anyway. They moved in the manner of sleepwalkers, took their seats without enthusiasm and the bus resumed its steady pace down the road.

Other vehicles came and went as the day wound on. The bus to *Comfortzone* was tempting, but Prudence suspected that if she went there, she would never want to leave. *Obfuscation* had such a complex route displayed that nobody could figure out if they should take it or not, and *Hewhohesitates* seemed lost. *Ifwisheswerehorses* had several beggars eager to ride, and *Mindlessbureaucracy* came past again and again until Prudence began to suspect it was just giving its long-suffering passengers the run-around.

Then there were the *Love* buses. Prudence found them particularly amusing, with destination signs proclaiming *Romance* and their drivers grinning like anxious clowns whenever somebody showed interest. Shade E. Deals was not the only person with a hungry expression! Some of the seedier ones even had *Romance—via Drunkenlust* on their displays. For some reason not many women wanted to go that route and certainly not the ever-prudent Prudence.

Then late in the day a *Love* bus came into view that was slightly different. Its driver wore the usual earnest expression, but the bus's display sign read: *Mutualfulfillment*.

Prudence was intrigued despite herself and watched as the untidy vehicle came to a stop in front of her. The driver, a middle-aged man with a beard and wearing braces on pants that looked a size too large, went to the door but struggled to open it.

"Try pulling it instead of pushing it," said Prudence, trying not to smile.

"Huh?" he replied, "Oh…yeah." The door opened easily, and the driver and Prudence regarded each other. He was wearing two different socks, but to his credit they were both the same colour.

"*Mutualfulfillment*?" she queried. "I'm not familiar with that place. Shouldn't this bus be going to *Romance*?"

"Well," he replied, looking up at the sign and thinking for a moment, "I guess you're right. This bus is heading for *Romance*, like all the others. At least that's the plan. But personally, I'd like to go a bit further than that."

"Oh?" said Prudence wryly. "So, you're hoping to reach *Commitment* then? Perhaps go all the way to…*Matrimony*?" She emphasised the last word as if it might be something distasteful to him.

The Driver, however, did not take the bait.

"Er, yes and no," he responded. "They're actually part of *Romance* and only a short distance from where we are. Plenty of people go to those places. To be honest they're a bit overrated though. I spent twenty years living in *Matrimony* and was bloody miserable most of the time. No, I was thinking of somewhere more challenging."

Prudence was reminded of her own unhappy stint in *Matrimony* and wondered what on Earth could be more demanding than that.

"I see," she said, even though she did not. "So where are you going with all this?"

The driver looked at her blankly and said, "Didn't you notice?" He pointed to the bus's destination sign.

Her eyes followed his finger to: *Mutualfulfillment*—via *Intimacy.*

Something in Prudence retreated from the sign, as if it were somehow naked, and she struggled to mask her discomfort.

"*Intim…*" She started to say it, then abandoned the attempt. "I thought that was part of *Matrimony?*"

"Yeah," he replied, "So did I—for a long time. But one day

I finally realised that Matrimony and Intimacy can be miles apart. You can be in one of those places for years and never even glimpse the other."

Prudence could certainly relate to that. She looked past him at the bus's interior. The floor had been vacuumed without enthusiasm and various items were scattered about the interior. A photo of three young women with a faint resemblance to him was sitting on a pile of books, and a pen sketch was draped over the dashboard waiting to be finished. Presumably while he was driving.

"And your name is?" she said, giving him a restrained smile.

"Strugg," he replied, wiping ink from his hand before extending it. "Strugg Lingartist."

"Prudence," she replied, hesitating for a moment before accepting the handshake. His hand was a bit nervous, but there was sincerity in the way he shook her little paw, and she was grateful that no ink came off when she withdrew her fingers. "Been travelling this way for long?"

"The *Love* route? No, this is my first week. Truth be told, I didn't do much preparation. A bit eager to get started."

"How's it going so far?" she said, noticing that the bus was new but already had a dent on one fender.

"Met some nice people. They weren't interested in going for a ride, but that's okay. I'm happy just to talk. Early days."

He had an intense way of staring at her face that Prudence found a bit off-putting, and she turned her eyes back to the bus. Then she noticed the artwork on the dashboard was a portrait. It was a pleasant drawing, as if the subject had been viewed with optimism.

"So," she replied, "You're a fine artist."

"Don't know about the 'fine' part, but yes, I do art."

"As a hobby?"

"No, I'm a professional," he replied, "Hard to believe, but yes, you can make a living as an artist. Mostly cartooning, there's not a lot of money in painting pictures."

"Oh," said Prudence, intrigued. "Cartooning? That must be interesting."

"It can be," replied Strugg, picking dried ink from beneath bitten fingernails. "Though it's more about ideas than art. Do you do anything creative?"

"As a matter of fact, I do," she said, pulling a note from her bag. "I like to write poetry sometimes while I'm waiting."

"Really?" he said, reaching for the note. "Can I see what you've done?"

Prudence was suddenly reluctant but saying no would have made her appear rude, so she handed it over.

He read the poem with a solemn expression that was broken occasionally by a small smile.

"That's very good," he said at last, handing it back to her as if it was a bouquet of flowers. "Impressive."

"It's based on a Shakespearean verse," she gushed, reddening at the compliment, and feeling like she needed to confess to a copyright infringement. "Um, do you write any poetry yourself?"

"As a matter of fact, yes," he replied, retrieving a sheet of paper from a pile of old notes, and handing it to her. "Did this when I was travelling some years ago. It's a bit maudlin but should give you an idea of what I can do."

Prudence read it through and agreed that it was gloomy, but it was also sincere. Its careful verse was in stark contrast to the rumpled paper and the rough scrawl of the writing. She noticed a date on the page as she handed it back.

"You wrote this thirty years ago. You must have quite a collection by now."

"Alas," he replied, "Once I stopped travelling, the poetry stopped as well. This is the only one I have left from those days. The rest are missing in action somewhere." He indicated his filing system and shrugged.

"Perhaps you just need to find inspiration."

"Yes," he replied in coy agreement. "Don't happen to know where *Inspiration* is by any chance? I can't find it on my GPS."

"No," said Prudence, sounding more dismissive than helpful. "Maybe you're looking in the wrong place."

"You can say that again," he said casting his eyes around the bus shelter. Several people were now waiting. Most of them were too engrossed in their phones and magazines to return his gaze, but the elderly lady caught his eye, and they shared a little smile and nodded to each other.

"So," he said at last, turning back to Prudence, "Been here long?"

"No," she exclaimed as if put on the spot. "Er, I mean... well, yes for a little while. But I don't want to rush into anything."

"Sounds sensible. I thought about doing something similar. Sit back and wait to see what comes along, but then impatience got the better of me." He patted the dent on the bus. "Better a journey plagued by mistakes than no journey at all."

Prudence sniffed. "There's a big difference between adventure and misadventure."

"Not with me. Order meets chaos every day."

He leaned against the bus only to have it roll forward.

"Never a dull moment," he added, disappearing into the cab to pull on the handbrake.

Prudence noticed he had dropped his owlish facade and was now wearing the clownish smile of so many other Romance drivers but in his case, it appeared to be the real person rather than a mask.

"So, Mr Lingartist…"

"Strugg."

"You have no real idea where you're going but are determined to get there."

He considered that for a moment before replying, "That's as good a description as any."

"How can any girl resist that?" She said, trying not to roll her eyes.

"I'm a master of seduction," he replied, pulling at his elastic suspenders to make his pants bounce up and down.

The conversation did not get any better as the morning turned into afternoon, but Prudence no longer noticed the other buses that came and went. Nor was she worried by the intense way he looked at her, having concluded that she was being viewed with the same optimism as the dashboard drawing.

For his part he was relishing her displays of indifference, answering each snide comment with a playful dig or something that made no sense at all. When hours had passed, and they were now standing only centimetres apart he smiled and took her hand.

"So, would you like to join me? You never know, if we go far enough, we might even find *Inspiration*. And I can't get to *Mutualfullfillment* on my own."

Prudence froze and looked down. Her fingers were in his, her right foot was on the bus step and her body was leaning forward as if fully intending to go with the offer. But the space between the curb and the bus now yawned beneath her like a gap between two high buildings and she recoiled with horror.

Strugg felt her hand slip away, saw the warmth disappear from her eyes and watched her feet retreat to the safety of the bus shelter. He appeared stunned and awkward in that moment, like a knight intent on rescuing a princess only to have her push him out of the castle, lock the door, lower the portcullis, and pull up the drawbridge.

They stood regarding each other once more but divided now by an impossible distance. Prudence put her hand to her face as if to restore the diffident mask she was wearing at the beginning of their conversation but found an offended one instead.

"You just want us to get a room," she said at last, for want of something better.

Strugg also found his offended mask but no words came out of it.

She then added, "Another time perhaps."

"Yes,' he replied after a prolonged silence, "Another time."

He closed the door, gunned the engine, and pulled away from the kerb at full speed, as if keen to get as far away as possible.

"Well," said Prudence with a haughty laugh as she returned to the bus shelter and sat down, "That was interesting."

"Indeed," replied the old woman, taking off her glasses to clean them for the umpteenth time. "Not tempted?"

"Oh, for a moment," she admitted. "But going on an adventure with no clear route or destination isn't my idea of fun. I'd rather keep my feet on the ground, thank you."

Prudence looked around to see if their conversation was

being overheard, but they were alone. Night had fallen and the bus shelter was empty. All the other passengers had found what they were looking for. She turned back to the old woman.

"Have you been here long?"

"Yes, my dear, a very long time."

They sat in silence until Prudence announced in a tone that was more forced than cheerful, "Oh, well, it pays to be fussy and tomorrow is another day. There's always something better."

The woman finished cleaning her glasses and restored them to the deep indents on her nose.

"Yes, my dear," she said at last, looking at Prudence through old sad eyes.